Fall in love?
Never! Never! Never!

Certainly not with the handsome Marquis of Trouvaine! Yet, on more than one occasion she had experienced strange stirrings—a sudden rush of blood in her veins, or a quickening of the senses.

Just recently, when the carriage horses had shied back from an aggressive hound, she had felt a strange thrill when his supporting arm came around her.

"No," she resolved, "I have more sense than to fall in love with His Lordship."

But, could she help herself?

**Millions of women
love Harlequin Romances**

**Millions of women
trust Harlequin Romances**

NOW

**Millions of women
can find that same love,
that same trust, in the**

NEW
HARLEQUIN
HISTORICALS

HARLEQUIN HISTORICALS bring you all the romance
and suspense, all the intrigue and mystery,
the excitement and adventure of an age long past.

HARLEQUIN HISTORICALS have the deep love and
sentiment you look for in Harlequin Romances.
They are about people you will care about. They
bring you other worlds and other times—all against
a background of pure romance.

Historical romances with the Harlequin magic

It was a time of lavish costume-balls . . .
of masked ladies in delicate folds of lace
and dashing cavaliers in pearl-trimmed satin . . .
starry-eyed lovers cruelly kept apart
by the rigid rules of the nobility . . .
secret meetings in hidden, leafy bowers . . .
and the quiet, serene beauty
of everlasting love.

It was the age of romance.

Harlequin now brings you the age of romance

It was a time of wicked conspiracies and dastardly plots . . . of virtuous ladies abducted by the all-powerful lords of the nobility . . . vicious highwaymen and scheming villains . . .

It was an age of threatening intrigue and swashbuckling derring-do, when strength and swordplay were all that counted, and right and wrong were as nothing.

But, it was also a time of pure romance.

Eleanor and the Marquis

Eleanor
and the Marquis

JANE WILBY

Harlequin Books

TORONTO • LONDON • NEW YORK • AMSTERDAM • SYDNEY

Harlequin Historical edition published September 1977
ISBN 0-373-05001-1

Originally published in 1977
by Mills & Boon Limited

Printed in Canada

CHAPTER ONE

No two cousins could have been less alike, both in appearance and situation. Yet despite this they had remained soul companions since the time when they were old enough to play together, either in the modest gardens of the Parsonage, or the far more gracious grounds of Ropestone Hall, home of Sir Thomas Doynsby and his wife, Philippa.

The Doynsbys' only child, Beatrix, though petted and pampered most excessively, was by no means spoiled, and this, declared the Reverend George Sherburn, was due entirely to the influence of his younger daughter Eleanor, who, even as a child, had never been known to evince one spark of envy regarding either her cousin's looks or her superior station as the daughter of a wealthy country squire.

"It's such a shame that Eleanor is always cast into the shade by my Beatrix," Aunt Philippa would say when, having arrived at the Parsonage in her chaise, she would stay to partake of tea in the small saloon which looked out on to a vegetable plot at the side of the house. "Yet the dear girl remains her own sweet self, never desiring that which she knows she cannot have. Thomas and I have always said how fortunate we are that Beatrix has such an amiable companion as Eleanor."

Eleanor and her Mama would exchange glances at this, Mrs Sherburn's eyes kindling with suppressed anger, but those of her daughter merely reflecting amused resignation. She did sometimes wonder what would be her aunt's comment should she inform her that she was quite happy with what nature had been kind enough to bestow upon her, that she actually preferred her own dark ringlets to her cousin's golden tresses, that she rather liked her own brown eyes – although she had always admired the vivid quality of Beatrix's blue ones, just as she had admired her cousin's lovely white skin which, Aunt Philippa would constantly remind her niece, was the envy of all the young females who attended the local assemblies. However, Eleanor was more than content with the touch of peach that highlighted her high cheek-bones and pointed little chin. And she had no desire for a rosebud mouth, although here again she had to own that it added enormously to her cousin's attractiveness.

"My Beatrix has the figure of an angel," Aunt Philippa would declare. "She is bound to make a brilliant match!"

"Eleanor's waist can be spanned by a man's two hands," Bertram, Eleanor's young brother, would swiftly retort, should he happen to be present when his aunt remarked on Beatrix's figure. "Let me show you!" And he would lift his sister high above his head, just to demonstrate his developing strength.

"It's not seemly for a brother and sister to act with so little decorum," Aunt Philippa would say with a frown. "I do deplore horseplay, and watching you two together makes me feel glad that we have no son to torment my darling Beatrix like this."

At which Mama and Papa would exchange glances; they were well aware that Bertram was the envy of Sir Thomas and his wife.

"I'm sure you're right about the horseplay, dear Philippa," the Vicar would say in his best pulpit tones. "Children, that's enough."

As for Mama, she too would admonish her son and

daughter ... but only when her sister-in-law was there, never in her absence.

The sisters-in-law were friendly enough and yet, beneath the surface, there was, on Philippa's part, a certain measure of condescension towards her husband's sister and her family. It was a well-known fact that Charlotte could have done much better for herself than marry the Vicar, but it had been a love match, and although Charlotte's rejection of the attentions of Sir William Smithson was a disappointment to her parents, they had allowed her to marry the man of her own choice.

Eleanor, highly romantic – she secretly read the stories in the *Ladies' Monthly Realm* – hoped that her own parents would be equally tolerant when, and if, she herself should fall in love.

"I expect your Mama and Papa will allow you to marry whom you yourself choose," sighed Beatrix when, one cold and dismal afternoon in January, she had been brought over in the chaise and left at the Parsonage while her mother and father went into town to do some shopping.

"I sincerely hope so, Beatrix." Eleanor bent over her embroidery, concentrating on the pattern. "I can't even begin to imagine what it must be like to marry a man of someone else's choosing."

"I am expected to make an advantageous alliance." There was anger in Beatrix's voice and, catching it, Eleanor glanced up swiftly, a question in her eyes.

"But surely you're happy at this? You've always known what is expected of you, Beatrix, dear. In any case, I have often heard you say that you'll make a brilliant match."

Beatrix glanced away; she and Eleanor were sitting on the couch in the saloon where, in the large low hearth, a cheery fire blazed.

"And so you, like Mama and Papa, and in fact everyone I know, have taken it for granted that I'm resigned."

"Resigned?" frowned Eleanor who, being a highly intelligent young lady, sensed at once that Beatrix was in the grip of some kind of problem.

"Resigned to marrying into the ton!"

Eleanor's eyes opened very wide at this extra show of temper.

"We have always known that you'll marry into the ton."

Beatrix turned; to her amazement Eleanor saw a tear hanging on her eyelashes.

"I'm in love," she cried tragically. "With Hugh Sommerville!"

"Hugh –!" Eleanor almost dropped her embroidery. "Impossible!" she exclaimed. "You're funning me!"

"Do I look as if I'm funning you?" The blue eyes were shadowed, the pretty rosebud mouth quivering. "I met him at the last assembly in York – you weren't there, remember?" Eleanor merely nodded, impatient for her cousin to continue. "We danced and talked –" Beatrix spread her hands. "We fell in love right away."

Eleanor said, a trifle fearfully,

"You've been seeing one another?"

"Whenever we can. Eleanor," she entreated suddenly, "will you help us to elope?"

"Elope!" Eleanor felt herself go pale. "No, Beatrix, how could you think of anything so shocking? What about your Mama –?"

"Mama is *all ambition*, Eleanor! I want to live my own life!"

"In poverty?" returned her cousin softly.

"Yes!" with defiance and determination. "I don't care about that! I want to marry Hugh Sommerville!"

"Well," said Eleanor practically, "you can't. So I strongly advise you to forget all about him. Next year you'll be going to London to make your debut. There you will meet all the eligible bachelors, one of whom will offer for you—"

"I don't care if a Duke or a Marquis should offer for me. I want only Hugh!"

"Nonsense! If a Marquis should offer for you then your Mama would see to it that you accept him." As for a Duke — Eleanor did not think that Beatrix, despite her fragile beauty, could manage to gain the interest of anyone quite so exalted as this.

"Oh, I wish my situation was like yours, Eleanor! Nothing spectacular is expected of you. You'll marry for love, and be happy ever afterwards."

Eleanor's mouth twitched in spite of herself.

"So you too read the novels from the lending library?"

"Mama would be so angry if she knew."

"Of course; so would mine. But I manage to read them in secret." A small pause ensued. "I expect it's all those romantic stories that have caused the trouble, putting ideas into your head. But you must forget them, Beatrix. Not for you the poverty of a smallholder's wife —"

"He's a yeoman farmer!"

"He calls himself that, but you know very well the meagre extent of his lands."

A tear fell on to Beatrix's cheek.

"So you won't help us to elope?"

"Most certainly not!"

"You always said you'd be my friend whatever happened," Beatrix reminded her accusingly.

"I am your friend."

"If you were a *true* friend, you'd leave no stone unturned in order to ensure my happiness."

"And what about the consequences of such an act on my part?"

"Oh . . ." Airily Beatrix flicked a hand. "It might cause

a tiny rift between our families at first, but it would all die down quite soon."

"I should be in disgrace with everyone, Beatrix."

"If you were clever, no one would be aware that you'd assisted us."

"It so happens that I'm not clever at arranging elopements, seeing that I haven't had any experience."

"Now you're being hateful with me," complained Beatrix. "I haven't a friend in the whole world except Hugh!" she cried. "I wish I were dead!"

"Beatrix, dear," said Eleanor soothingly, "I can't possibly be a party to your eloping. You must know that you are not being at all reasonable. I *am* your friend, you know this. I wouldn't be your friend were I to help you to fall into disgrace. Why, everyone would be thoroughly shocked if you were to elope. And in addition your poor Mama would break her heart."

"So it doesn't matter if my heart's broken? That does not appear to trouble you at all, Eleanor."

A deep sigh escaped from Eleanor's lips. How could she deal with a situation like this? She ought by rights to tell her own Mama what was going on, and leave her to decide whether or not to inform her sister-in-law of the danger. But Eleanor knew she would never be able to adopt that course, and yet, if Beatrix should decide to elope, then she, Eleanor, would carry the weight of a guilty conscience for the rest of her life.

"I don't know what to advise," murmured Eleanor at last. "To tell your Mama, in the hope that she might allow you to marry Hugh —"

"Would be futile and you know it."

"You'll have to forget him, Beatrix."

"I won't!"

"Your Aunt Lucy in London is expecting to bring you out next season."

"Why should they assume that I want that kind of life? I just want to marry my Hugh and settle down to a country life. I shall enjoy being a farmer's wife, no matter what you or Mama or Papa might believe to the contrary."

Eleanor said nothing, aware that no argument on her part could move her cousin. However, she could not marry this small farmer, that was certain. It would not do at all – the squire's daughter as the wife of a man who once worked for Sir Thomas but who, having inherited some small acreage of land, had decided to set up on his own.

"I'll ask the maid to bring some tea," Eleanor offered, putting aside her embroidery and rising from the couch.

"If Mama calls tomorrow, which I expect she will, you won't say anything?" Beatrix was asking the question as Eleanor returned from the kitchen. "I know you won't, but I'd like your promise?"

"I promise," returned Eleanor at once, unable to be angry with Beatrix at her lack of trust, since the girl was far too unhappy already.

As it happened, Aunt Philippa did not call until the end of the week, and by this time Eleanor was seriously considering going along to see Hugh Sommerville and pointing out to him that to continue seeing her cousin was only courting trouble.

"My Beatrix gets lovelier every day," declared Aunt Philippa, and this caused Eleanor to look sharply at her. So it would seem that Beatrix was already coming round to her old self, for she had certainly not been looking very pretty when she was confiding her problem to her cousin. In fact, her face had been so drawn that Eleanor had feared her Mama would question Beatrix as to the reason for this decline in her looks. "She will undoubtedly make a most suitable match, for once she gets to London and attends the balls and routs and assemblies she is bound to attract all the young men! Her Papa and I are expecting her to attract a Marquis at least, but even a Duke is not an impossibility, not with her beauty."

"Our sister-in-law does not know the difference between beauty and prettiness," the Vicar said when Philippa had made her departure. "She certainly aims high for her daughter," he added with a sort of mild satire. He and his wife were sitting by the window, looking out on to the "wild" garden which, they declared, was far more pleasing to the eye than the more formal garden which had been planned by Sir Thomas's grandfather and where the real products of nature had been ruthlessly killed off. The truth was that the Vicar's income did not run to more than one gardener and, therefore, it pleased him and his wife to say that they liked their garden to look natural.

"Philippa *is* certainly aiming high for Beatrix," agreed Charlotte. "I hope she isn't going to be disappointed."

Eleanor, sitting at the back of the room, her embroidery needle idle in her hand, listened intently to this conversation and presently she heard her Mama say, with a trace of regret in her tone,

"It isn't any use my hoping for a brilliant marriage for Eleanor. I expect she can do no better than her sister."

"She's comfortable, our Augusta, so I don't know that I want anything better for our other daughter."

"Algernon's so dull, though. I fear that Eleanor would find life a bore married to someone like him."

Algernon, frowned Eleanor, who had never cared much for her sister's husband. He owned a small estate in Derbyshire but to hear him talk he might have been a member of the landed gentry. How Augusta managed to put up with his boastings Eleanor had never been able to understand.

"I know I cannot expect much," she said to herself, "but heaven forbid that I have to make do with a man like Algernon Edwards!"

The next afternoon Beatrix came over to the Parsonage;

she talked all the time about her Hugh, trying to inveigle Eleanor into forming some plan which would simplify the alliance. Becoming really apprehensive now, Eleanor was once again tempted to drop a hint to her Mama, leaving the rest to her, sure that she would know how to act.

"Your Mama said that you were growing more lovely than ever, so I thought you must be getting over your infatuation for Hugh," she said, looking intently at her cousin for any signs of the harassed expression she had encountered before. Beatrix did look a trifle upset, but there was something about her that suggested she was not now quite so unhappy as she had been previously. Was she determined to run off with this Hugh, even without the help she was trying to enlist from her cousin?

"I shall never get over Hugh," almost snapped Beatrix, going on to add that it was no infatuation and never had been. "I love him and he loves me, so we shall marry – yes, in face of all opposition!"

"If Hugh is as determined as you, then why does he not approach your father and ask his permission to address you?"

"You know very well why!"

"Beatrix," said Eleanor in her most persuasive voice, "you really must look at this situation more unemotionally. Hugh is too poor at present to support a wife who has been used to every luxury as you have. Think what it will be like to do your own housework, to do everything for your husband and, later, your children. It wouldn't work, Beatrix. You'd become so dreadfully unhappy even after the first few months."

"Months! What a cynic you are, Eleanor!"

"I happen to have known you since you were born, remember. So I should be in a position to know what you are like. You adore the luxury of being waited upon, Beatrix, and having your own private chaise – your father's

chaise, of course. If you were married to Hugh you'd
have to travel on the stage-coach – if you travelled at all,
that is."

"It's no use your trying to put me off marrying Hugh.
I will *not* give him up!"

"If your father finds out –"

"Then the explosion will come. And I might as well tell
you, Eleanor, that I should not be at all sorry!"

Brave words, thought Eleanor but, having known her
cousin for over seventeen years, she was under no illusions
as to whether or not she would stand up to her father.
Sir Thomas would tell her what she must do – and she
would do it.

"I expect that just because you're two years older than
I am you feel you're far advanced in wisdom," Beatrix said
with faint sarcasm as she was leaving. "Well, I have always
owned to your superior brain, Eleanor – in fact, I know
that your Papa considers me an addle-head –"

"No, dear Beatrix," Eleanor began to protest, but her
cousin interrupted her.

"And in many ways he's right. As I've just admitted, your
brain is better than mine, but that does not mean, Eleanor,
that you have more wisdom!"

When Beatrix had left Eleanor mused for a long while
over the situation, feeling on the one hand that she must
not let Beatrix down by divulging what she knew, but on
the other hand aware that it was her bounden duty to
prevent her cousin from making this disastrous alliance.
Had it been Eleanor herself who had fallen in love with
Hugh everything would have been all right; she was used
to helping her mother with various household duties, as
her father's small income restricted the family to limited
staff. Also, a man like Hugh Sommerville would have been
quite a suitable "catch" for someone in Eleanor's circumstances who had never known the good things of life.

"I think I ought to go and see Hugh," she murmured thoughtfully. "It seems to be the only thing I can do."

However when she eventually did ride over to see Hugh, the journey proved a waste of Eleanor's time. She saw at once that he was so much in love with Beatrix, it would be pointless to ask him to break off the liaison.

"I see no reason why we shall not be blissfully happy," he said. "After all, love is a surer basis for happiness than the wealth in the man or woman's coffers."

"Beatrix is an only child, Hugh," Eleanor reminded him significantly.

"So you assume I'm marrying her for her money?"

"No, but there are many people who will think that."

"Let them."

"My uncle won't ever permit a marriage between you," she asserted gravely. "I tell you, it will be far more prudent for you to give one another up."

When at length she came away she had not been able to extract any promise and she was seriously debating whether to tell her Mama and leave the rest to her. Yet she still hesitated, feeling she would be a traitor to her beloved cousin.

However, Eleanor was to be spared this, for it transpired that the news of Beatrix's visits to her lover's home came to her father's ears, causing a major upheaval, with Sir Thomas raving and his wife being almost in a state of collapse. The upshot of all this was a speedy message to Lucy, Dowager Duchess of Carandale, imploring her to take Beatrix under her wing.

"I've to go to London," wailed Beatrix when eventually she was allowed out – but at the same time escorted on her short journey to the Parsonage. "I've told them I won't go on my own! I want you with me, Eleanor. Please say that you'll come?"

"Me?" ejaculated Eleanor, a dazzling vision of balls

and theatres and routs passing before her. "But it isn't possible," she then added as a more practical picture supplanted the other. "For one thing, my Papa could not provide me with the clothes and other necessities for that kind of sojourn in London."

A small pause followed; Eleanor, noting its strangeness, waited for what was to come. She did not know what she expected, but she was certainly unprepared to hear her cousin say,

"Mama suggests that you might be glad – I – er – mean," stammered Beatrix, aware of her tactlessness, "Mama thinks you might go as my abigail . . ." Beatrix's voice trailed off slowly as she noted the expression on her cousin's face.

"Your abigail, eh?" Her brown eyes glinting with fire, Eleanor looked straight at her cousin. "Inform my aunt," she went on frigidly, "that poor as we are in comparison with her, my Papa would never for one moment permit me to adopt the role of a servant!"

Beatrix coloured painfully, and fidgeted with her fingers.

"I'm sorry, dear Eleanor. You see, it's b-bad enough h-having to go to Aunt Lucy – leaving my dearest Hugh, and I c-can't go without you."

"I'm sorry," returned Eleanor implacably. "You'll have to leave me out of it. We don't mind being poor; as you know it's a circumstance we three children accept without rancour, glad that our Mama and Papa married for love. Nevertheless, in spite of our poverty we are a proud family, as you should very well know, Beatrix." Eleanor's head lifted, revealing the beautiful white curve of her neck, and the proud set of her head upon shoulders that sloped just sufficiently to be declared perfect.

"I can't go without you," cried Beatrix, miserably. "Please come with me?"

Totally aloof now, Eleanor shook her head, setting her

mouth in a line which matched to perfection the rest of her bearing.

The following morning Beatrix's Mama and Papa visited the Parsonage with their daughter, and while the two girls walked in the garden their parents went into conference in the parlour. The approach of the Doynsby carriage along the frost-flecked country lanes had been noticed by Eleanor who, speculating on the reason for this early morning visit of her aunt and uncle, had immediately sought out her Mama and given her a brief outline of what had transpired the previous day. Amazed and angry, Mrs Sherburn had been quite unable to contain herself.

"I cannot think why my sister-in-law should even have brought forward such an idea! Did you tell Beatrix that your Papa would never, *never* countenance such a scheme?"

"Yes, Mama, I most certainly did."

"And yet you say the carriage is approaching?"

Eleanor nodded her dark head.

"I thought it best to warn you," she said, adding that had it not been for this visit she would not have troubled either her Mama or her Papa with the intelligence that her Aunt Philippa had suggested her niece take on the role of abigail to her daughter.

"I wish that you had informed me yesterday," Mrs Sherburn said, still in the same wrathful tones. "I didn't even know that Beatrix was going to London this year. I understood Philippa to say it was next year."

"The visit's been brought forward," said Eleanor, turning away and hoping her Mama would not inquire any further into this.

"But, why?" These two words dashing her hopes, Eleanor turned back and looked into her Mama's angry eyes.

"Please, Mama," she said quietly, "will you wait and let Aunt Philippa tell you all about it?"

Mrs Sherburn frowned, as well she might, for it was clear that some mystery existed. However, she agreed to wait, seeing that it would be only a few minutes in any case, but she did go on to say that she would have to make a great effort in order to be civil to her sister-in law if she so much as mentioned that Eleanor should adopt the role of abigail to Beatrix.

"How she dared to make the suggestion I cannot understand! We are poor, but not servile – and never shall be!"

Just at this moment Eleanor's Papa entered the room and Eleanor slipped away, to put on some warm clothes so that she could walk in the garden with her cousin.

"I'm sorry about yesterday," was the first thing Beatrix said as Eleanor joined her after responding most coldly to her aunt's greeting. "I made you angry, and so I was miserable and unhappy all night."

"You're definitely going to London?"

Beatrix nodded dejectedly.

"I shall have to do so." She swallowed convulsively. "It was awful when they found out about Hugh," she added with a shudder.

"I can imagine," returned Eleanor sympathetically. "I know what a temper Uncle Thomas has."

"I shall never be able to marry Hugh ..." Beatrix's voice failed as she started to cry. "But I shan't marry anyone else, so sending me to London is a waste of both effort and money."

"You'll forget Hugh in time," Eleanor told her gently. "It would never have done, as I told you right at the first."

"I expect *you* will marry for love," was Beatrix's pettish response to this. "But then your Mama knows she can't expect very much for you since your expectations are so small."

"That's true," agreed Eleanor without the least trace of

rancour. "In any case, I shall never go anywhere where I could meet any eligible bachelors who have titles and wealth." Up till now no mention had been made by either young lady regarding the reason for the visit to the Parsonage of Beatrix's parents. Eleanor had no intention of broaching the subject and Beatrix was most reluctant to do so. "Nevertheless," mused Eleanor almost to herself, "I must admit that I should like it above anything if I could go to London and mingle with the ton." Despite her outward resignation that she would never see the London scene, she had not stopped thinking about it since Beatrix had suggested she accompany her. To have gone as Beatrix's companion would have been wonderful, and although it was only a dream, Eleanor had dwelt on the possibility, ignoring such mundane things as the expenses involved. To any young lady in Yorkshire the glamour of a London Season was the zenith of delight. There were balls and theatres, military reviews, assemblies and private parties – and numerous other diversions. Light-hearted flirtations were also part of the glamorous scene, but Eleanor, being the Vicar's daughter, did not think she would indulge in a flirtation, even given the unlikely opportunity.

Mama sent for Eleanor as soon as her visitors had departed.

"They put the proposition to your Papa and me," she informed Eleanor. "I was civil, but more than that I was not!"

"And Papa?"

"As always he was graciously polite; nevertheless, he more than made his point that our daughter, though neither so well-connected nor so set up in finery as Beatrix, was far above taking on the role of servant to her. To which I added," went on Mrs Sherburn grimly, "that our daughter had more pride in her little finger than Beatrix had in her whole body!"

"Mama! Oh, but you weren't so rude as that!"

"I said, my dear, that I was civil."

"Well, that certainly doesn't sound like civility to me."

Her Mama said no more. Much later Eleanor was in the small saloon, mending one of her brother's stockings, when she again glanced through the window to perceive the approach of her uncle's carriage. This time Beatrix was not with Sir Thomas and his wife ... and this time Eleanor was sent for almost as soon as the greetings had been exchanged by both couples.

After being told the reason for this visit Eleanor could only stare, unable to believe that she had heard aright.

"Me – go to London as Beatrix's companion?" Her soft brown eyes went to her Papa's face. "We can't accept this offer," she said, thinking of the expense.

"We wouldn't have sent for you had we not discussed this matter and decided that we could afford to let you go with Beatrix," Mama said with gentle affection.

"Discussed it? But when?"

"Your Mama made the suggestion this morning," Papa explained in his slow calm tones. "Your aunt and uncle promised to consider it, so naturally your mother and I have been discussing it also."

Eleanor looked questioningly at her Mama.

"You suggested it even without knowing if we could afford it?"

Papa smiled now and said,

"Both your Mama and I are thrifty, my dear. We do manage to save despite our apparent poverty."

The faintest hint of sarcasm here, decided Eleanor, looking at Sir Thomas to see what effect this had upon him. He seemed faintly uncomfortable. However, his wife, brisk now that the decisions had been made and all were agreed that Eleanor should accompany Beatrix to London as her companion and not her abigail, began to expound on the delights awaiting the girls – but then immediately dampened everything by saying,

"However, do not go there with the hope that you might be fortunate and make the kind of marriage we expect from our little Beatrix. Keep in mind, Eleanor, dear, that it cannot be your destiny to marry into one of the Houses." She turned a warning eye upon her sister-in-law. "I have a strong suspicion, Charlotte, dear, that you are harbouring an optimistic vision of Eleanor capturing a man of consequence?"

Eleanor noticed that this caused her Mama to blush, which in turn brought a dainty hint of colour to Eleanor's own cheeks.

"I do not think it's a total impossibility that our daughter should attract a man of consequence," said Mama with a touch of defiance.

Aunt Philippa was shaking her head. She said rather sadly,

"This isn't fair of you, Charlotte – not fair to dear Eleanor." She turned to her and added, "Do not heed your Mama, Eleanor, for it is the worst thing when a person's hopes are built up, only to come crashing to the ground. My Beatrix will undoubtedly be able to have her pick from many London beaux, but you –" She stopped to glance rather pityingly at her niece. "Gentlemen prefer Beatrix's type, brunettes being out of fashion in London Society at present, and so you can expect to be outshone by Beatrix. I know I'm speaking rather plainly, but I feel it my duty to warn you not to go on this sojourn cherishing high hopes of attaining anything splendid in the way of marriage." She paused a moment to see if anyone had anything to say. Eleanor remained silent; her Mama dared not speak for fear of saying something insulting to her sister-in-law. As for Papa and Sir Thomas – they both sat staring in front of them, Sir Thomas plainly still uncomfortable even though – Eleanor suspected – he was mentally agreeing with everything his wife had to say. "It's possible that you might manage to attract the attention of a half-pay officer," continued Aunt Philippa in her customary condescending tones. "In which case, dear Eleanor, it will be your duty to accept him, if only for your parents' sake." She paused again, examining Eleanor's flushed face. "Promise me that you'll forget what your Mama has just said, for I cannot *bear* to have you hurt, dearest Eleanor."

"I promise," returned Eleanor with a swift glance in her Papa's direction. His face, normally so placid, now revealed a hint of anger. However, he sat back and allowed the women to talk between themselves, and this they did — about such things as ball gowns and morning dress and Almack's and the Drawing-room.

"Now that it has come to it," said Aunt Philippa, "I am delighted that my Beatrix is to enter the Polite World rather sooner than we had planned. You see, if her debut is successful, then she will be *settled* sooner than we expected."

"By a successful debut," interposed the Vicar, "I see that you mean she will find a wealthy husband."

Lady Doynsby looked doubtfully at him, not quite sure just how to take that remark.

"I fear you're being sarcastic, George," she accused. "I might add that my dear little Beatrix is *sure* to find a wealthy husband."

"So you have told us many, many times before, my dear."

An hour later Mrs Sherburn stood by the window, watching the carriage move away.

"What a set-down it would be for Philippa if you, my love, did happen to make a brilliant match as a result of your sojourn in London."

"It isn't possible, Mama, darling," returned Eleanor. "Please do not cherish any hopes of a miracle such as that."

Her Mama gave a deep regretful sigh, nodding her head.

"Yes, you're quite right, my love, it isn't possible, not with your insignificant expectations." She paused a moment and then, "Mr Melville ... he's presentable, and he has a comfortable income. He has a *tendre* for you, and you could do worse."

Eleanor swallowed hard. She knew that she ought to be considering one of the several young gentlemen who, having met her at the local assemblies, had begun to show an interest in her. Her brother wanted to go to Oxford; she knew that it was her Papa's ambition that he should attain this desire. It was incumbent on her, then, to relieve the strain on the family income by finding herself a husband.

"I cannot marry Mr Melville," she returned with some distress. "When I return from London I shall consider one or other of the young men who are interested in me ..." Her voice died as she swallowed again. "You and Papa married for love," she said, not really meaning to say anything like that.

"We were fortunate, my dearest Eleanor. But this does not happen very often."

"I do understand, Mama – and as I have said, I'll think about marriage just as soon as I come back."

CHAPTER
TWO

THE Dowager's house in Cavendish Square was a noble edifice which, with its vast entrance hall and grand staircase, left Eleanor speechless the moment she entered it. Beatrix, more used to this kind of luxury, merely looked around with studied indifference and requested the footman to announce her arrival to his mistress.

"The drawing-room's on the first floor," she told Eleanor. "I expect you'll find it strange after the best parlour at the Vicarage."

Not only strange but quite overpowering, thought Eleanor when, having been conducted there, she stood for a moment on the threshold, staring around the spacious apartment with its carved ceiling embellished with mythological subjects, and its high walls hung with tapestries. Aunt Lucy came forward to embrace her niece, drawing her to her ample bosom and planting a resounding kiss on her pale cheek.

"My dear Beatrix! My, but you grow more pretty every time I see you. I think it was a good idea of your Mama's to decide on your come-out this year, as you will never be lovelier than you are now. Alas, a woman's youth is so short-lived!" The Dowager turned then, and as her eyes looked into the face of Eleanor they suddenly widened and then stared for fully thirty seconds, a sort of amazed disbelief in their depths. Beatrix, unaware of anything strange in her aunt's behaviour, muttered an introduction and then turned away. The Duchess extended a hand which Eleanor took in hers, smiling and saying,

"I'm honoured to meet you, ma'am. And please may I thank you for your generosity in taking me as a guest into your home?"

The Duchess smiled at last.

"Very prettily said, my dear. Might I express the hope that you will enjoy your Season in London." She was still staring, seeming to be taking in every line, every classical contour of Eleanor's face; then her eyes moved to her high forehead, to the dark glory of her ringlets, those at the front peeping from beneath her high-crowned bonnet. "I believe you will enjoy it," she added on a strange and cryptic note. "And it could prove to be of advantage to you, Miss Sherburn ..." The Duchess's voice trailed slowly to silence; it was plain that she had fallen into a thoughtful mood. Puzzled by her manner, Eleanor glanced for inspiration at her cousin, but Beatrix was merely standing by the window, staring absently at the tall trees outside. "Yes," murmured the Duchess, "it could prove to be of advantage to you." At this Beatrix did turn, evidently having caught the gist of her aunt's words at last.

"Advantage to Eleanor?" she queried. "In what way, Aunt Lucy?"

"Your cousin could make a notable marriage –"

"Mama says that dear Eleanor must not cherish hopes of anything like that, simply because she is to be brought out. You see, Aunt Lucy, her expectations are of such slight consequence that she cannot be expected to be noticed by anyone of importance. Mama seemed to think it would be most unkind if she were encouraged to hope for a miracle."

The Dowager's straight black eyebrows were raised.

"There are times," she said coldly, "when your Mama annoys me!"

Much put out of countenance, Beatrix murmured an apology, then, turning to Eleanor – who was herself experiencing some embarrassment – she said meekly,

"There was no offence meant, dearest Eleanor; you do know that?"

"But of course," returned her cousin instantly. "Think no more about it." She looked at the Dowager. "I shall enjoy my sojourn in London, ma'am, but I shall most certainly not harbour any unlikely hope that I may attract a man of consequence." She was smiling, one of her most attractive features, and her tones were quiet and resigned. She hoped she had made it clear to the Duchess that she did not aspire to compete, even in the smallest degree, with her cousin. This visit to London was made specifically for the purpose of establishing Beatrix comfortably in life – this by marriage to a gentleman of consequence and property, and Eleanor's role was nothing more nor less than that of companion to her cousin.

The Dowager was frowning heavily ... and there was a strange expression indeed in her pale blue eyes. She was thoughtful, too, and for no reason at all Eleanor gained the impression that she was away in the distant past, re-living something that had happened, something which was far from pleasant.

"We shall see," she murmured to herself at length. "This girl's the image –" Pulling herself up with a jerk, the Duchess smiled. "I must say that I like your modesty, Miss Sherburn. It's obvious that you've always been overshadowed by your golden cousin here?"

Put out by this plain speaking, Eleanor blushed and averted her head.

"That is true, ma'am," she admitted quietly.

"Did it never dawn on you that your particular type of beauty might become all the rage in London?"

"Ma'am," said Eleanor, aware that her cousin was becoming angered by her aunt's words, "you must know better than anyone that blondes are all the rage in Society here."

"At this present time." Glinting, those blue eyes now, and tight the mouth. "There is nothing so fickle as fashion," she said, again speaking to herself. "How very gratifying if I could change it –" Once more she pulled herself up; once more her expression was changed by a smile. "You do happen to be a beauty, Miss Sherburn, even though you yourself might not know it –"

"A beauty!" exclaimed Beatrix, suddenly unable to listen in silence any longer. Having had her own attractions praised as often as Eleanor's had been deplored, she had grown accustomed to the idea that there existed a vast distinction between her own looks and those of her cousin. Eleanor was "passable", Lady Doynsby had asserted, but her Beatrix was beautiful. "Mama has always said . . ." Beatrix allowed her voice to fade as she caught her aunt's expression. "I'm sorry," she murmured, again adopting that meek tone of voice. "I was most rude – or, I mean, I was about to be," she added apologetically. "Please forgive me," she begged of her cousin.

"Of course; in any case, it's of no consequence." Light through her voice sounded, Eleanor was, for the first time ever, annoyed with her cousin. To be constantly reminded of the difference in their appearances was becoming so boring that she felt she would not be long before she put an end to it by asking her cousin outright not to refer to it again. However, remembering her position as a guest in the Dowager's house, Eleanor saved anything she had to say until later, when she and Beatrix would find themselves alone.

Refreshments were brought in, and after the girls had partaken of them they were conducted to their respective rooms by footmen. Eleanor's room was so handsome an apartment that a somewhat undignified gasp rose to her lips even as she crossed the threshold. The high walls were hung with delicate pink paper, the curtains at the tall windows were of a deeper shade, and made of the finest velvet. An Axminster carpet covered the floor, while the sofa and chairs were upholstered in deep crimson satin. A four-poster bed was draped prettily with muslin which matched the flouncing around the dressing-table.

"If only Mama could see it!" she was exclaiming to herself as soon as the door had closed behind the footman. " How she would enjoy sleeping in such a noble apartment as this!"

Eleanor, being not only of a sunny disposition, but also a girl who easily adapted to new situations and surroundings, knew that she would soon be feeling comfortably at home here in this gracious house. That she was one of the most fortunate young ladies in the whole country had been firmly established in her mind since the moment she was informed that she would be accompanying her cousin to London for the Season. Eleanor was grateful to Beatrix for wanting her, to Sir Thomas and his wife for granting their daughter's request, to the Dowager for her kind consent to bring her out. But Eleanor was especially grateful to her Mama and Papa because, for them, the expense of fitting her out in clothes suitable for her entry into the Polite World must have eaten drastically into their savings.

Eleanor's meditations were interrupted by a tap on the door. A maid in starched cap and apron bobbed a curtsey immediately the door was opened.

"My name's Eva, Miss. I'm to be your personal maid and dresser. Shall I unpack your trunks and bandboxes now, or would you wish me to come back later?"

A personal maid ... Having done everything for herself

for so long Eleanor would rather have done without the services of a maid. However, as she could not think of sending the girl away she smiled and said yes, she could stay and unpack the trunks and bandboxes now.

"Have you been in London before, Miss?" enquired Eva conversationally as she put one of the bandboxes on a chair.

"No, Eva, this is my first glimpse of the Fashionable World."

"Is it, Miss?" The girl smiled wisely, just as if to convey to her new mistress that she knew all there was to know about the Fashionable World. "Then you are in for a treat, I'm sure."

"Yes, I believe I am." She contrived to speak coolly and calmly, but inside – oh, she did experience the most exciting feeling of anticipation!

"The Duchess is giving a ball for your coming out?"

"For my cousin's coming out, really," confided Eleanor, having already taken a liking to Eva, who was a slender, pretty girl, with auburn curls and big green eyes. She was about nineteen years of age – just her own age, thought Eleanor. "You see, I have come only as companion for my cousin, Miss Beatrix."

"But you will be brought out as well," returned Eva confidently, and then she left what she was doing and came closer to her new mistress, saying in a confidential tone of voice, "The Duchess enjoys chaperoning young ladies who are making their debut. She's been widowed so long that she gets bored if she has nothing to do, and when she knew you were coming with her niece she was delighted. 'Just think, Eva,' she said to me, '*two* young ladies to take about and introduce to the ton! It will make me feel quite young again'. I recall when she brought out another niece of hers, and also the ward of the Marquis of Trouvaine – a rare beauty, she was, I can tell you! But she did have designs on marrying her guardian, which was rather stupid of her because the Marquis is known to consider marriage a bore and a bind. He likes his opera-dancers too much to settle down to only *one*!"

Eleanor, wondering vaguely if this gossiping by the maid was quite the thing, decided to fall silent in the hope that Eva would also lapse into silence, concentrating on her task a little more. However, after a moment's meditation Eleanor found herself becoming interested in the fact that the Dowager would converse freely with someone so very far beneath her, and she felt compelled to ask Eva about this.

"The Duchess chats to you in a friendly manner, then?"

"I'm her favourite," smiled the maid. "My parents worked for her when her husband, the Duke, was alive. But they died within a month of one another and the Duchess was so upset that she took me under her wing, giving me a good education, and then, later, a position in her household. I'm her personal maid usually, but she has given me to you for the present."

Eleanor frowned on hearing this.

"But why?" she wanted to know.

"I must admit I was puzzled myself at first," admitted Eva, lifting out a pretty dress of sprigged muslin and hanging it in the wardrobe. "But I now believe it's because she's taken an extraordinary liking to you, Miss. Of course, I shall continue to dress her Grace's hair, but she wants me to devote most of my time to you." Eva stopped, and Eleanor perceived that a blush was spreading over her cheeks. "You see, Miss, I am considered to be one of the most gifted coiffeurs in all London. There are many ladies of the Quality who have begged the Duchess to part with me."

Eleanor had become thoughtful. It went without question that Beatrix's aunt had taken a deep liking to her, but

why? Eleanor glanced at the maid, who was busy with
another dress – a puffed-sleeved, high-waisted gown of
sarsnet with crepe trimmings and flounces round the bottom
of the skirt. Should she question the maid a little? It seemed
all wrong, of course, but Eleanor's curiosity being well and
truly aroused, she was having the greatest difficulty in
containing it. She decided to say cautiously,

"It would seem that the Dowager is anxious that I should
be made to look – well – rather attractive?"

"Very attractive, Miss." Eva shook out another dress,
this time of Berlin silk trimmed with ribbons and lace.
"Her Grace has *something* on her mind," the girl went on
to confide. "I know that look in her eyes – that faraway
expression, Miss. It's always there when her Grace has some
design afoot. A strange one, is the Duchess, but I love her,
Miss, and am grateful, as you can understand, seeing what
she's done for me?"

"Yes, indeed! It would be the shabbiest thing if you were
not overflowing with gratitude, Eva."

"I know it, Miss." Eva paused before lifting up the lid
of another trunk. "About that something on her mind I
mentioned – I cannot be sure, of course, but I somehow
think she means to make you all the rage –"

"Oh, no! This is ridiculous! Eva, I do believe you are
bamming me!" And yet even as these protestations escaped
her Eleanor was recalling the strange behaviour of the
Duchess, reflecting on her assertion that she, Eleanor, was
beautiful, reflecting also on the strangeness in her voice
when she had murmured the words, "We shall see,"
after Eleanor had implied that she had no hope of attracting
a man of consequence. The Duchess had also mentioned
something about Eleanor's particular type of beauty becoming the rage ... had said how gratifying it would be if she,
the Duchess, could change the existing fashion, which was
the preference for blondes.

"I'm not bamming you, Miss," Eva replied with a serious inflection to her voice. "I feel that my mistress would like you to take London by storm."

Eleanor shook her head, distressed now as she thought of Beatrix, who should be the star while she, Eleanor, was supposed to keep in the shade.

"Why should your mistress like it if I were to take the town by storm?" she had to ask, even though she felt that this conversation was becoming far too intimate. "I am only enquiring about a probable reason, you know, Eva – I am not for one single moment considering such a possibility, since it is far too absurd that a Nobody like myself would ever take London by storm."

"A Nobody has done it before," Eva reminded her with a calm and knowing smile. "As for a reason for my mistress's desire, I cannot answer you, Miss. All I can say is that the Duchess is of a rather eccentric disposition, and it's often said of her that her every act is either to please herself or to annoy someone else."

To annoy someone else ... Eleanor was to recall these words within a very short time, and to have an explanation for them. Meanwhile, she was to be entertained most enjoyably in listening to the murmurings of the Dowager when, during the evening, she and her cousin sat demurely on the sofa in the drawing-room while the old lady began making up the list of guests she intended to invite to the coming-out ball.

"I shall send cards to the Booths and the Savilles – then there's the Earl of Crooknall, a most eligible bachelor – though his Mama is a great bore with her ailments. Lord and Lady Solvay – they have two sons, both of whom are well set up. The Viscount and Viscountess Heron who give the most famous parties. The Muschamps also, and the Hamlades. The Fairfax crowd – Sir John, his wife and their son and daughter. Their assemblies are famed, as are their dinner parties." She stopped, and a smile lit her lined face as she looked across towards the girls sitting in polite silence on the couch. "You'll meet scores of young men who will take your fancy, Beatrix, and in the process you'll forget all about this most unsuitable farmer you've been doting on."

Beatrix went red.

"I love him," she faltered, flicking a finger to her eyes as if she feared a tear might fall.

"Rubbish, child! No sensible girl falls in love with the first man she meets!"

"He isn't the first man I've met, Aunt Lucy," returned Beatrix firmly but respectfully. "But he's the one I want to marry. I love him," she added with a catch in her voice.

"Fustian! Marriage, my child, and romance are poles apart!" With a negligent wave of her thin hand her Grace dismissed Hugh Sommerville as if he were no more important than the flunkeys who would be in attendance at the ball. "Now, where was I? Ah, the Walworths – they can do you a spate of good socially, since they're related to all the Houses of note. Then we must have Lady Jersey, and perhaps that odious Princess Lieven, both of whom can send you vouchers for Almack's."

"Almack's," breathed Eleanor, an awed expression in her lovely brown eyes. "I had never aspired to enter the portals of that most exclusive of London clubs, ma'am."

"It's imperative for any debutante's success. You must know – both of you – that you will suffer a serious set-back if you are not admitted to Almack's."

"We will?" frowned Eleanor, wondering what her Papa would have to say to anything like this. "But how absurd, ma'am."

"I agree wholeheartedly, my child." The Dowager looked hard at her, examining every line and curve of her face. "I have a suspicion that the frivolities of our London scene will not always find favour with you – the result of your up-bringing in a Vicarage," she added, but with a touch of amused irony in her voice. "However, you're here to enjoy yourself, so you must turn the blind eye to anything that displeases you."

"It would seem that people here live for pleasure alone?"

"Indisputably," agreed the Duchess. "Take the Regent himself – his tailor is of far more importance to him than his Prime Minister. Prinny lives entirely for pleasure, and the only times when he exerts himself are in the arranging of enjoyment for himself and the Carlton House Set."

Eleanor's frown deepened; she was not at all sure that she was going to take to these people whom the Duchess was inviting to the ball.

Beatrix, having been silent for the past five minutes or so, gave a small sigh and said,

"For my part, I'd sooner live in the country, enjoying the quiet life. I'm sure that all this round of parties and other entertainments must become tedious to me after a while."

"Not when you get used to it, my love," stated her aunt. "I've yet to meet the young lady who hasn't managed to fall into the London scene without much difficulty." She transferred her gaze to Eleanor. "You, my child – I sincerely hope you're going to throw yourself into the pleasures the Season has to offer?"

"Of course," responded Eleanor readily. "I intend to make the most of my good fortune in coming here. It's only that I find it difficult to assimilate the fact that a person can make or break another's career."

At this the Dowager's face hardened, bringing about a dramatic change in her appearance. She looked positively wicked, thought Eleanor with a little inward gasp. However, when at length the old lady spoke there was nothing in her voice to support the idea that she had been angered by some distant memory.

"It's understandable that you find it difficult, my dear; nevertheless, that's how it is, I'm afraid. Take for instance the great Brummell; he most certainly can make or break a debutante's career."

"So I have heard," nodded Eleanor. "It's said that if he should happen to treat a young female with indifference then she will be shunned by the ton."

"Decidedly she will. On the other hand, should he condescend to afford her ten minutes of his time, then the Polite World will accept her without hesitation; she'll be inundated with invitations to balls, parties, assemblies – oh, everything that happens to be going." A pause ensued; that hardness came over the Dowager's face. "There have been women who from time to time have exerted this same power ..." The old lady was drifting, swept away by her own thoughts – thoughts of the past, Eleanor felt sure. "Yes, and *one woman* in particular ..." The voice of the Duchess was like a whiplash suddenly, and the pale eyes seemed to catch on fire. "*One woman* who was able to ruin my sweet little –" The sudden halting of the voice was followed instantly by a smile as the Dowager realized what she had said. "Yes," she resumed, briskly putting pencil to paper, "*we must* invite my friend Mr Brummell!" The name was written down, while the two cousins on the sofa looked at one another with puzzled expressions on their faces.

"As I happen to count Beau Brummell as one of my admirers, I expect he will do as I bid him and see that you are set firmly on the first rung of the ladder of success." Her eyes, instead of settling on her niece's face, had settled upon Eleanor's – with a most unfathomable and disconcerting stare. A strange sensation swept over Eleanor; she knew that the old lady was hatching some sort of plot, and that the plot would involve Eleanor herself. "I must send a card to Lady Haldene," said the Dowager, once again returning her attention to the notepad in her hand. "Perhaps your Mama has told you about her?" she presently inquired of Beatrix.

"No, Aunt, she hasn't," replied Beatrix indifferently.

"Isn't she the lady whose routs and assemblies have made her famous?" queried Eleanor.

The Dowager nodded her head.

"Even her house is famous because of her entertainments. It's as well-furnished as the house of any nobleman, and the hostess herself is as dignified as any lady in the land."

"I have heard that she is very beautiful also?"

"Extraordinarily beautiful."

"I have heard it said that her assemblies are among the most lavish in all London – that they sometimes even rival those of the Court?"

The Duchess smiled at these knowledgeable pronouncements and said,

"That's correct. So you do manage to get some of the London news up there in Yorkshire?"

Eleanor smiled and said yes, they did have small items of news trickling through from time to time.

"But, living as we do right out in the country," she added, "we don't get the news until it is history, as you might say."

The old lady nodded before giving her attention even yet again to her list of guests.

"Lord and Lady Vandersley," she mused, slightly frowning. "I don't know that they can do you much good socially, since their parties are the shabbiest events imaginable. Their cousin, Lady Fieldman, now, ... yes, I shall certainly send her a card. The Holdings give magnificent entertainments, and so do the Poynings. Not Charlotte

Fitzpayne, since she is another whose entertainments are invariably shabby." She looked down the list, silently continuing to add names, and then, looking up again, she said with a deep sigh of satisfaction, "Lastly, there is the Marquis of Trouvaine, my nephew."

The philanderer, recalled Eleanor, thinking of the conversation she had had with Eva. The man who preferred opera-dancers because *one* woman would obviously never satisfy him.

"Your nephew?" Beatrix, plainly deciding it was time she opened her mouth, wrinkled her brow as this question was phrased. "I don't think I have ever heard of him?"

"Perhaps your Mama didn't consider it necessary to mention him," returned the Dowager with a hint of amusement in her voice. "He's something of a rake, you see. Nevertheless, he and I manage to get along famously, both being of an unorthodox turn of mind –" She stopped on noting the look of puzzlement on her niece's pretty face. "We're more than likely to do something quite outrageous," she elucidated for her benefit. "Something that no one else would think of doing."

"Are you? What?" Beatrix was not in the least interested in any answer she might receive, and Eleanor did wonder just how long she would be enveloped in this fit of the doldrums. As for Eleanor herself – this interlude with the Duchess, whom she was growing to like more and more with every moment that passed, was exceedingly diverting and she was making mental notes so that she could relate it all when she wrote to her parents.

"No matter," was the Dowager's half-impatient reply. "Now, as to my nephew, the Marquis. He might just consider a ball of this kind to be a dead bore and a dreadful squeeze, but he shall come all the same, for if he should dare to refuse I shall threaten to cut him out of my will completely."

"If you are inviting him with a view to making a match between him and me," said Beatrix pettishly, "then, I beg of you, please do not trouble. My dearest Eleanor will assure you that I have told her I shall not consider an offer from a Duke, even!"

The Duchess actually laughed.

"You can set your mind at rest about the Marquis, my love. He will never offer for you – or for anyone else, for that matter. He's reached the age of thirty-two without losing his freedom and he'll not lose it now, I can assure you. There isn't a female of marriageable age who hasn't been paraded before him by her doting and ambitious Mama, but he treats them all the same – with a kind of arrogant derision."

"He sounds horrid to me," pouted Beatrix, flushing a little because of the set-down she had received from her aunt. "I shouldn't be surprised if he's a bachelor merely because no one will have him."

"He's the country's most eligible and most pursued gentleman; he's handsome and rich, being related to all the Houses that matter. He owns a fine mansion in St James's Square and the family seat in Kent. He's a notable Whip, an Arbiter of Fashion – being second only to Brummell himself."

"You mean," interposed Eleanor, "that other men follow the fashions which he sets?"

"Of course. And not only in clothes. If Justin, Marquis of Trouvaine, decided to carry a bright red knitted reticule about with him, then all the Tulips of Fashion would do the same."

"How odiously disgusting!" exclaimed Eleanor before she could stop herself. "Why do men follow like sheep, I wonder?"

"That, my dear, is something which even I cannot answer. And in fact I do not have the least desire to do so, since, like you, I find such foppish imitation disgusting in the extreme."

"I wonder why you invite him at all," said Beatrix. "I'm sure he will make himself horridly objectionable."

"I invite him because of his usefulness," replied the Dowager with unashamed frankness. "He, like Brummell, can by a word or look, make or break a girl's career." Her eyes became fixed upon Eleanor's face. Eleanor was drawn to the very clear conclusion that the Duchess was once again in the past, her mind having strayed, her eyes having become glazed. "Should Justin favour you with one of his rare smiles, or his company for a few moments at one of the fashionable assemblies, then you will be made."

"And supposing he snubs me?" said Beatrix, a curious expression in her eyes.

"Then you are almost lost, my love."

"I see . . ." Beatrix glanced away on noting the light in her cousin's eyes. That she was planning to treat the Marquis in such a manner that he would snub her was more than plain. Such an action would assuredly bring about the collapse of all the plans her doting parents had made for her. And because she loved her cousin, and in addition felt that she owed a great debt to her aunt and uncle for allowing her to come here with Beatrix, Eleanor decided to have a talk with the Marquis, just to put him in the picture as it were, and to beg him not to snub Beatrix but, on the contrary, to favour her with his smile, so that she would swiftly rise to fame in the Fashionable World to which her parents had so hopefully sent her.

"I do not look forward to the discourse with him," she was telling herself that night when, after being assisted by Eva, she was undressed and lying awake in the big four-poster bed, and pondered what she would say to the Marquis. "However, it must be done, no matter how odious I find the man." And she added later, "Thank goodness I don't have any need to toady to him for any favours for myself, for I know already that he is the most arrogant, self-opinionated, supercilious dandy – a man whom I shall dislike intensely the moment I set eyes on him!"

CHAPTER
THREE

IT was to transpire that all Eleanor's predictions regarding her opinion of the Marquis of Trouvaine were to go by the board. Instead of disliking him on sight, she was so taken aback by his good looks, his noble bearing, his impeccable taste in dress, that she could only gasp in admiration, and silently declare him to be the most attractive gentleman upon whom she had ever set her eyes.

Introduced to him the day following her arrival at the Duchess's home, she found herself having the greatest difficulty with her composure. She did however manage to retain a cool exterior as she gave him a half-smile and expressed herself in a similar way as she had earlier greeted his aunt – that was, she told him she was honoured to make his acquaintance. His faintly humorous smile was neither heartening nor disheartening, since to Eleanor it revealed nothing.

The Marquis returned his attention to Eleanor after having had a few words with his aunt, speaking to her with cool civility as he inquired about the journey down from Yorkshire to London.

"We came by my uncle's travelling carriage," she informed him with a smile. "It was pleasant because the weather was fine and sunny, though cool. And the beds at the posting-houses were very good indeed."

"It's the fashion, my dear," interposed the Dowager with some amusement, "to say the beds were *tolerably* good."

Eleanor blinked, not quite understanding why she should

not give praise where praise was due. Her Papa had always taught her to do this and she felt it was right.

"And how exciting it was to have the groom holding a pistol as he sat beside the coachman," said Eleanor, feeling it would be safer to change the subject rather than argue with her hostess. "But we didn't meet with any highwaymen," she added regretfully.

The Marquis's dark blue eyes regarded her with a curious expression as he said,

"Am I to understand that you would have welcomed the appearance of a highwayman, Miss Sherburn?"

"For myself," she said, "I would rather have enjoyed the experience. However, my cousin, Beatrix, might have been afraid, so it was as well that we weren't accosted."

The Marquis began to raise his quizzing-glass, intending to survey her through it, but for some reason he changed his mind, a circumstance for which Eleanor was grateful, since she would have found such a scrutiny more than a little disconcerting.

"You will have observed," said the Duchess with a chuckle, "that my protégée is a somewhat unusual young lady?"

"Oh, no, ma'am! I am quite ordinary!"

The Marquis's lips twitched. He chatted for a while and then,

"Where," he inquired of her, "is this cousin of yours?"

"Resting, sir. She was out shopping in Bond Street this morning." She stopped, aware that already he was looking bored. To confirm this idea she saw him raise a long, slender hand to suppress a yawn. As the action appeared to be a snub, she excused herself and left the room, making her way up another flight of stairs to her cousin's bedroom. Here she knocked gently on the door, unwilling to wake Beatrix if she should be asleep but more than a little eager to describe the Marquis to her.

"Who is it?" came the pettish enquiry. "I'm resting!"

"It's only me – Eleanor."

"Come in, then."

"The Marquis is in the drawing-room with your aunt," Eleanor informed her excitedly as, moving over to the bed, she sat down right on the edge. Beatrix was lying on the coverlet, her cheeks damp and red. "You've been crying," observed Eleanor with some concern. "Dearest Beatrix, do try to forget Hugh and make an effort to enjoy yourself."

"I want to go home!"

A sigh escaped her cousin.

"Shall I tell you about the Marquis?" she asked patiently. Beatrix looked intently at her.

"You said you weren't going to like him, but judging from your expression he has found favour with you?"

"Indeed yes! Oh, Beatrix, he is the most outstandingly handsome gentleman! – with very dark blue eyes and black hair, and the most distinguished bearing, being so tall – over six feet two inches, I'm sure! Can you imagine my feelings when finding myself face to face with this Nonpareil?"

"What were your feelings?" Beatrix was easing herself up into a sitting position; she appeared to have lost a little of her indifference, and a faint gleam of curiosity showed in her vivid blue eyes.

"I was speechless with wonder!"

"It isn't like you to become excited over a *man*."

"But if you were to see him! Such a fine figure, Beatrix – lean and strong. And such broad square shoulders that do not require the padding which my brother has had sewn into his newest coat."

"You say he's good-looking. Is he anything like my Hugh?"

Eleanor hesitated.

"Well . . . no, Beatrix –"

"You're saying that Hugh isn't good looking, aren't you?" accused Beatrix, an angry glint in her eye.

"I'm sorry, dear, if you have taken it that way; it was not meant to be. You see, there is no comparison, Hugh being fuller in the face. His lordship's features are lean and long, and his nostrils rather thin. His eyes have a sort of piercing quality that can be quite disconcerting, as can the whole personality of the man, for it is undeniably magnetic—"

"Magnetic?" repeated Beatrix derisively. "Where did you find an expression like that? In one of your books, I suppose," she added, answering her own question. "Well, if you've told me all this in the hope that I shall become interested in him, then you're wasting your time."

"You know very well that it was not my intention to encourage you to be interested in him. Your aunt has said that he is a confirmed bachelor."

"I shall snub him," asserted Beatrix in fractious tones, "and then I shall be ruined socially and there'll be nothing for it but for Aunt Lucy to send me back home."

Eleanor bit her lip.

"I don't want to go home yet," she said.

"I'm sorry if you consider me selfish, dear Eleanor, but I shall do all I can to get back to Hugh as soon as possible. I feel that I was a coward to be forced to come away, against all my own inclinations. You had better enjoy yourself as much as you can during the next few weeks, for I am sure we shall be leaving for Yorkshire by the end of the month." Eleanor said nothing and after a moment her cousin informed her that she preferred to be alone. "I expect you will find something to do, dearest Eleanor," she added, obviously experiencing some degree of guilt. "You did bring some of your books with you, I remember."

After leaving her cousin's bedroom Eleanor decided to stroll in the garden, the weather being unseasonably warm, with the sun shining down from a clear blue sky. She was walking along a path close to the south wall of the house when suddenly she stopped, aware that the Duchess and her nephew were now in a small saloon situated on the ground floor. They were talking and the Duchess's voice floated out quite clearly through the open window.

"I've asked you three times, you tiresome creature, what you think of my protégée!"

"The provincial?" The Marquis's voice was dry. "Not much. Have you any particular reason for asking me what I think of her?"

Not much ... Eleanor's cheeks burned with anger and mortification. To think that she had gained an attractive impression of him!

"I intend to make her the rage, Justin –"

"The rage!" he ejaculated. "You must be bamming!"

"No such thing! She has beauty –"

"Brunettes are not in fashion, you know that as well as I. This other chit – your niece. She could be successful, if she's all you say she is."

"Golden curls and bright blue eyes! I want the fashion changed, Justin!"

Eleanor, realizing she could not move away without being seen from one of the three windows in the room, pressed against the wall and tried not to eavesdrop. But it was impossible, since both the Dowager and her nephew were speaking in clear, finely-modulated voices.

"Changed?" echoed the Marquis. "What on earth for?"

"I've just informed you that I intend to make Eleanor the rage."

A small silence followed and then the Marquis spoke.

"Come on, then," he encouraged, "Out with it. What's your game this time?"

"Lady Mildred Tiernay is bringing out her grand-daughter this Season."

Another silence followed this announcement.

"I see. Revenge, eh?"

"Exactly."

"The provincial – she's the image of Catherine, you say?"

"You've seen my daughter's portrait in the Gallery, so you should have perceived the likeness?"

"To tell the truth I didn't take much notice of the provincial just now. I didn't know then what you were plotting, remember."

"My little daughter seemed to be in that room again when, after greeting Beatrix, I glanced up into the face of her cousin. The same black curls, the same beautiful brown eyes, the same heart-shaped face – Oh, but they could have been identical twins!"

"Except that Catherine would have been over forty years old by now – had she lived." The Marquis seemed to move away from the window as he spoke, for his voice became less clear. However, he soon returned to his aunt's side and Eleanor heard him say, "I know you've told me the story a couple of times but I must admit I wasn't particularly interested. Perhaps you'd like to repeat it again?"

"It was just twenty-two years ago. Mildred Tiernay was bringing out her daughter. Brunettes were in fashion; my Catherine was obviously going to be the rage. She had set her heart on the Duke of Leybourne's eldest son, Jocelyn. He had already been doting on her and everyone expected their betrothal to be announced sometime during the Season. But at that time Mildred Tiernay was the number one leader of fashion; dashing wife of a brilliant politician, she had established herself securely at the top and all she said or did was followed without question by the ton. She had always hated me, and I her. Jocelyn was the biggest catch of the Season and she was furious that he favoured my Catherine. And so she changed the fashion. Brunettes were out, she decreed – and she managed to enlist the help of two men who were leading Society, whose iufluence was at that time similar to that of Brummell and yourself today." The Dowager stopped and Eleanor waited for her nephew to speak. Her heart was racing, for she saw now that she was going to be used by the Duchess, who was determined to be revenged on her enemy.

"The Duke's son married Lady Tiernay's daughter?"

"That's right."

"He couldn't have cared very much for Catherine, after all," was the Marquis's logical statement.

"He was led by fashion. The two men I have mentioned – both of whom are now dead – let it be known that brunettes were not fashionable; they snubbed my child, made sneering remarks about her beauty, nicknaming her the Gypsy, with the result that she began to be shunned by the ladies of fashion – this after she basked amid an army of admirers. The invitations dwindled. Jocelyn was weak, I admit, but he was swayed not only by the fact that Catherine was being shunned by the ton, but also by his Mama who pointed out that with her as his wife he too would fall from favour."

"And poor Catherine went into a decline, from which she never recovered."

"As you know, she died at the age of eighteen and a half."

"Six months after the marriage of the Duke's son and Lady Tiernay's daughter – I think that is what you once told me?"

"Your memory serves you correctly."

"I can now see the explanation for your anger when someone attains the power to sway public opinion."

"It's natural that I become angry. However, it so happens that the two who now hold that power are Brummell and yourself. My nephew and my friend. I mean to use you both. George shall dance attendance on my protégée, and so shall you."

"Aunt Lucy," said the Marquis softly, "I hope that you are not giving me an order?"

"Be it an order or a request, you will heed it! Mildred Tiernay's granddaughter is a ravishing blonde ... and all set to take London by storm, so I am told, for there is none to come up to her. The Incomparable, they are calling her. I want her brought right down, as my daughter was brought down!"

"Is that fair to the girl? From what I myself have heard she is of a gentle, easy-going disposition."

"Then you have either heard a pack of lies or you've got the chit mixed up with someone else. Much as I want revenge I would not harm an innocent girl. Lady Isobel Bouchier, daughter of the late Duke and Duchess of Leybourne, is the most haughty, the most spiteful, the most ill-tempered creature you could ever meet! No, Justin, I have no pangs about what I'm planning to do."

"I cannot say that I want to be a party to it," said the Marquis, and by the inflection she heard in his tone Eleanor strongly suspected he was suppressing a yawn. "Women's foibles are not for me."

"I shall cut you off without a penny!"

"How many times have I heard that threat?" laughed the Marquis. "And how many times have I informed you, my dear aunt, that I have no need of your money?"

"You will if you continue frequenting those gaming hells!"

"I never lose much."

"You ought to settle down! How much did that diamond bracelet cost you?"

"How the devil do you know about that!"

"News travels. Which opera-dancer was it for? Not that long-faced chit I saw dangling on your arm at Vauxhall Gardens last August?"

"Since when have you begun frequenting Vauxhall Gardens?"

"I accompanied the Wedesleys; they had made up a party. I don't know what you find to amuse you in the place. I was intolerably bored, watching some odious man performing on a tight-rope. The fireworks weren't up to much, either. I was glad when it was time to leave – which was in the early hours of the morning."

Another laugh escaped the Marquis.

"It's time you gave up such frivolities, ma'am."

"I intend to – but not until I've brought this young female out. *And* made her the rage."

"You're quite determined, I see."

"You'll afford me your help?"

"My dear aunt ..." Eleanor heard no more, and she guessed that the Marquis had again moved away. She waited for a while, still afraid to move even though no further drifts of the conversation came out to her. At last she made a cautious attempt to leave her place by the wall. As she passed the window she could not resist peeping in. To her relief the Duchess and her nephew no longer occupied the room.

It was with mixed feelings that Eleanor dressed for the ball. By now she was fully convinced that the Marquis was intending to assist his aunt in her scheme to launch her into Polite Circles and to send her right to the top. She was to oust the Incomparable; she was to put blondes in the shade, to bring brunettes into fashion. Undoubtedly the idea of becoming the rage appealed to Eleanor, but as her first duty was to her cousin – whose parents had sent her to London for the sole purpose of making an advantageous marriage – Eleanor was naturally perturbed at the idea of blondes going out of fashion. However, it soon dawned on her that, pawn in the Duchess's game as she was, she had no power at all of her own. She supposed she could, by some subtle manoeuvre, turn the Marquis and Mr Brummell against her, but as that would be most disloyal to the Duchess, who had so kindly taken her into her home and promised to bring her out – this long before she had met her and conceived the idea of using her as an instrument of revenge – Eleanor decided against any action that could rebound on the old lady.

"Oh, Miss," gasped Eva when having put on her ball dress of Valenciennes lace, Eleanor stood before the long mirror, "you look like the Queen!"

"I hope not!" declared Eleanor with a grimace.

"You know what I mean, Miss! I've never seen any young debutante look so perfect as you!"

Undoubtedly Eleanor felt elated; it could not possibly be otherwise as, still staring with a sort of fascination into the mirror, she noted the way the gown clung to her figure at the top, then fell in delicate folds from her tiny waist. Dainty satin shoes peeped from beneath the hem. Her dark hair, gleaming with health and cleanness, fell in an enchanting disorder of curls on to one shoulder, while on the other side it had been drawn back and secured with a white satin riband intricately tied so that six small bows formed flower petals, in the centre of which was a flawless white diamond which the Duchess had insisted she wore. To Eleanor's surprise the Duchess had stood over Eva while this unusual hair style was being created, giving orders in rather abrupt tones, making the girl move a lock here and there if its situation did not satisfy her Grace.

"I want the immaculate style eliminated, Eva," she had said. "You must create a certain amount of disorder on this side. Miss Eleanor is to have a slightly wind-blown look."

"But, your Grace," protested Eva, faintly startled, "will that be quite the thing for so important an occasion as this?"

"If it's done by you, yes." And as this was more than enough to encourage Eva to go all out to produce a style that would please her beloved mistress, the result was breathtaking.

The Duchess returned to Eleanor's bedchamber just as her toilet was complete. Eleanor turned from the mirror; the Duchess stood very still, her pale eyes glittering with a strange mixture of pain and triumph. Eleanor knew without any doubt at all that the old lady was seeing her daughter, knew now the reason both for the gown of Valenciennes lace, and the unusual hair style. The Duchess could see her own daughter's image, standing there before her eyes. Compelled to break the silence, Eleanor said,

"Ma'am – may I thank you for this beautiful ball dress?"

The Duchess continued to stare, but at length she murmured,

"If it pleases you to thank me, child, then do so by all means. But there is no need, since I am deriving the greatest satisfaction from introducing you into the Polite World."

"The gown is indeed a most dazzling creation," Eva said when the Duchess had gone. "But you have many lovely clothes in your wardrobe, Miss."

Eleanor gave her a wry smile.

"I spent hours and hours having materials pinned about me before I came here. In York we have a Madame Fraville who, being a newcomer to the city, has not yet begun to make her charges in accordance with her gift as a dressmaker. She has a wonderful flair for design, and that is how I come to possess so many lovely gowns."

"You have been very lucky. Your morning dresses and riding clothes are of the finest materials and cut. And as for your afternoon dresses and evening wear – why, even her Grace could be put into the shade by some of the things you have."

"No," protested Eleanor, picking up a pretty little evening reticule of white silk trimmed with silver thread and hanging it from her waist. "I have nothing to compare with the expensive clothes worn by the Duchess!"

Eva merely shrugged, handed Eleanor a painted fan, then opened the bedchamber door for her to pass through.

"You'll be a sensation, Miss, "she said with a smile.

This prophecy – which only reflected that of the Duchess – was to prove to be correct. The Marquis, obviously pandering to her Grace's will, immediately upon his arrival bespoke Eleanor's hand for no less than three dances, while George Brummell did the same. Beatrix, who had earlier decided to indulge in a fit of the vapours, had been unable to remove the traces of her tears, and although she was dressed superbly, and with her golden ringlets gleaming, she was not her usual attractive self, a circumstance that troubled her cousin far more than it did the young lady concerned.

"I don't want to appear attractive," she snapped when Eleanor had made a tactful suggestion that she apply a cold compress to her eyelids in order to conceal the evidence of her tears. "In any case," added Beatrix with an all-embracing glance at Eleanor, "I'd never be able to compete with you!"

"Compete?" Eleanor spoke in tones of sudden distress. "We are not in competition, dearest Beatrix."

"All this was supposed to be for *me*!"

"And so it is ..." Eleanor allowed her voice to trail off to silence, aware that there was an element of hypocrisy in what she was saying, and not for the first time she was wishing she had not overheard that conversation between the Dowager and her nephew. Later, at the ball, when the cousins were again conversing, Beatrix said mulishly,

"My aunt has taken an extraordinary liking to you – but I don't care! I only want to go home!"

"Miss Sherburn. . ." The quiet voice of the Marquis broke into the conversation, and Eleanor turned right around, to stand before him, an enchanting picture of innocence and beauty. She did not smile, recollecting, as she did, his words when asked by her protectress what he thought of her.

"The provincial? Not much," had been his derisive rejoinder.

His eyes were now flickering strangely as they looked into her face.

"My dance, I think?" She nodded her head and the next moment he had encircled her waist as he led her into the waltz.

"How are you enjoying your first taste of London Society?" he enquired conversationally after a while.

"Very well, thank you, my lord."

"What is wrong with your cousin?"

"Wrong?" she prevaricated. "I don't know what you mean."

"I was given to understand by my aunt that she is in the doldrums over something?"

"That, sir, would not interest you," was Eleanor's rather cool reply. The Marquis held her from him, examining her expression as if he would read something from it.

"A mystery, eh?"

"Her Grace might give you an explanation, if you ask her."

The Marquis fell silent after this, but when a little time had elapsed she saw that he was leading her towards a door through which was a small saloon.

"Where are we going?" she wanted to know.

"I have a feeling that you find it rather stuffy in here. We shall sit for a while and you can partake of a glass of lemonade."

"I did not say it was stuffy," began Eleanor, when the

Marquis interrupted with the bland but somewhat impatient information that he and she were to be seen sitting together – solely because her protectress had ordained that this should be so.

"It will do you good socially," he ended, still with that trace of impatience in his voice.

He found her a chair, then went off to procure the lemonade. Glancing around at the other people sitting about, Eleanor saw that Lady Tiernay and her granddaughter were in the far corner. Eleanor had been more than a little surprised on hearing their names announced, upon their arrival at the ball, but it soon occurred to her that although the Duchess hated her, she would naturally invite her and her granddaughter to the coming-out ball of the girl she meant to make the rage.

And what a start her ladyship had given when she met Eleanor. She too was seeing the lovely Catherine, and although it was inconceivable that she was not exceedingly puzzled by what the Duchess had done, as yet she had no notion of the diabolical plot being hatched by her enemy.

"You are interested in her ladyship's tiara?" The gentle voice of the Marquis had a quizzical note to it as, after handing Eleanor the tall glass, he took his place beside her. "It's a dazzler, I must admit."

"But not in such excellent taste as your aunt's," Eleanor was swift to retort. "I would suggest that the diamonds in the Duchess's tiara are much finer in quality than those in Lady Tiernay's!"

The Marquis turned his head to look curiously at his companion.

"You're obviously fond of my aunt?"

"Naturally, my lord. She has been kindness itself to me."

The Marquis's lips twitched; it was not difficult for Eleanor to guess at his thoughts. He was thinking that the Duchess was working entirely for her own ends.

"Tell me about yourself?" he invited unexpectedly, sitting back and stretching his long legs out in front of him. "Your father's a Vicar, I understand?"

Eleanor nodded her head, marvelling at the way she was quickly becoming at her ease with him. This was surprising if only because of the derogatory way he had spoken about her to his aunt.

"Although I am told that it is unfashionable to disclose one's situation, I cannot say otherwise than that we are quite poor, and that I would never have come to London had it not been that my cousin Beatrix's parents had desired that I accompany her – on Beatrix's request, that was."

Again his lordship's lips twitched. Eleanor, looking sideways at him, thought again that she had never in her life encountered any man half so handsome as the Marquis of Trouvaine.

"It is as well, I think, that you mentioned your situation to me before mentioning it to anyone else. For I have a notion that my aunt would not want it to be generally known in Society that you are poor. I advise you not to mention it again."

"Oh, but I cannot say I'm an heiress," she protested. "That would never do!"

He almost laughed.

"Papa's influence, eh? Never must a fib cross his daughter's fair lips."

She blushed daintily.

"Now you are quizzing me, my lord!" she returned indignantly.

"Perhaps." He paused a moment. "You are quite diverting," he told her unexpectedly. "Quite out of the ordinary."

"Provincials usually are." This retort came unbidden and she automatically put a hand to her mouth. "I m-mean," she amended, noticing the swift, interrogating look he flashed at her, "that it's n-natural that they'll l-lack the polish of your London females."

He regarded her frowningly for a space.

"I'm not aware that I said you lacked polish – nor did I *imply* such a thing."

"No, my lord," was all she could find to say.

"Nor, to my recollection, have I used the word provincial this evening."

"No, my lord," she said again. She began sipping her lemonade, her eyes automatically straying to the over-dressed lady in the corner. Her granddaughter was no longer with her, having been claimed for a dance by one of London's most eligible bachelors, the Earl of Brockheath, heir to a Dukedom and a vast estate in Hampshire.

"Then where," persisted the Marquis, "did you get the word?"

"The word?"

A quick intake of breath revealed to her that her companion was experiencing some degree of impatience, and she turned to him, afraid that she had vexed him. This she must not do, because of her indebtedness to his aunt.

"Provincial," returned his lordship briefly.

Eleanor saw that his mouth was tight, his eyes glinting dangerously. Her heart gave a lurch; he was rather over-powering when in this mood, she thought – and forbidding also.

"I'm sorry, sir, if I wasn't affording you the attention that I should have been doing. Er – the word . . . I expect I merely used it because I happen to know that, here in London, people like me are referred to as provincials."

"I see." His voice was crisp and curt. She greatly feared he would rise and leave her, so ruining the effect which his aunt had planned.

"I do beg your pardon, my lord," she said meekly. "I hope you'll forgive me?"

He looked curiously at her. She held her breath, half expecting him to question her further. However, he allowed the matter to drop, not troubling to say whether he forgave her or not. After a while she decided to broach the subject of Beatrix, although she did have extreme difficulty in finding a sufficiently tactful way of saying what she had to say. She began by remarking, in a sort of chatty manner,

"I was telling you about my reason for coming to London."

"So you were." The Marquis's eyes had wandered to the woman in the corner. "It was as companion to your cousin, whose presentation was desired by her parents."

"Yes, that's right. Well, it's like this, my lord, Beatrix might not seem of an affable nature to you – when you speak to her, that is. But please don't heed any coolness she might display. It's only her manner, my lord."

The Marquis's dark eyes narrowed somewhat.

"You had better be a little more explicit," he told her. "I believe you are telling me to overlook this female's churlishness. If so, then you can save your breath, ma'am!"

Eleanor bit her lip.

"I'm afraid I have angered you, my lord."

"I am not in the habit of being given instructions by females, ma'am – "

"Please do not insist on calling me ma'am in *that* tone," she implored. "It has a most derogatory ring!"

She was plainly distressed, but if he saw this he chose to ignore it completely.

"You were saying, Miss Sherburn, that your cousin's manner is cool. It might interest you to know that young females aspiring to a brilliant London Season are not in the habit of treating me coolly!"

"You mean, sir, that you can make or break my cousin?

I know this," she continued before he could speak, "and that is why I am trying to warn you – "

"Warn, Miss Sherburn?" he interrupted in a very soft tone, and again Eleanor bit her lip. She was making a very poor attempt indeed to explain – in fact, she was strongly of the opinion that already she had done her cousin a disservice by broaching the subject in the first place.

As for Eleanor's opinion of the Marquis – well, she was fast strengthening her original idea that he was pompous and self-opinionated, that he was ever conscious of his superiority and position as one of the notable Corinthians who led Society. She felt that he was far too steeped in the frivolous ways of the ton, far too deeply aware of the power and strength of his influence upon those who – in Eleanor's opinion – were stupid enough to follow where he led. However, as it had to be accepted that he *was* able to exert his influence upon Society, it behoved any ambitious female not only to treat him with respect but even to adopt an attitude of humility when in his presence.

"I didn't quite mean it that way," said Eleanor at last. "Perhaps the word warn was misplaced."

"It was," agreed the Marquis coldly.

"Then I must apologise again," she said. She took another sip of her lemonade, but suddenly it seemed to taste like acid and she put the glass upon a small table close to her elbow. Opening her fan, she employed it gracefully to cool her hot cheeks. The Marquis looked on indifferently; she wondered if he were bored. "Shall we return to the ballroom?" she asked at length, because the silence had become oppressive, and because, even though she had not said all she had meant to say, she had no further desire to discuss her cousin. However, her companion was not satisfied; he wanted to know more about Beatrix. Surprised, Eleanor replied quite without thinking,

"She is desirous of earning your disapproval, my lord, so that she will be sent back home to Yorkshire."

"Why should she wish to return to Yorkshire, when she has come for her presentation?"

Eleanor hesitated a moment in indecision. And then, having made up her mind not to conceal anything, she remarked that it was plain that his aunt had not let him into the secret regarding the real reason for Beatrix's sudden appearance in London.

"You see, sir, she was not to have come until next year. But, having fallen in love with a gentleman far beneath her, she was sent off at once by her Mama and Papa in the hope that she would not only forget her Hugh, but would also meet someone more suitable to marry in London."

"I see." The Marquis subjected Eleanor to a stern censorious glance. "Why on earth didn't you tell me this in the first place – instead of floundering all around the subject like most of the simpering females I meet?"

"I'm sorry, sir," she responded meekly. "I thought to be a little restrained in the amount of information I imparted to you."

"You knew I had only to ask my aunt – if I were interested, that was."

"Will you be understanding now that you have been acquainted with the situation, my lord? Will you ignore any rudeness which Beatrix might exhibit towards you?"

His lordship was frowning heavily as he considered this.

"I shall probably give her a set-down she'll remember," he decided, "but privately." He noted the relief in his companion's brown eyes and his own eyes flickered with that odd expression she had surprised in them before. "I don't know why I should want to put your mind at rest like this," he added. "I expect I'm anxious to please that old villain of an aunt of mine, that is all."

"I would like to express my sincere thanks, my lord."

"Don't mention it, Miss Sherburn." His eyes had lost their hardness; a twinkle had appeared in their dark depths. "I've taken a load from your mind, judging by your expression?"

"Indeed yes," was her naïve reply. "I feared I had set you against me for ever."

He looked directly at her as she turned her face to his.

"You would have done – had it not been that I have no desire to upset my aunt."

She glanced away, aware of being snubbed. What an insufferable man he was!

Saved from finding a response to this by the appearance of the Dowager, Eleanor gave a deep sigh of relief and even managed to produce a smile when asked by her protectress if she was enjoying herself.

"Yes, ma'am, very much indeed," at which the Marquis raised an eyebrow as if questioning the truth of this.

The Dowager stayed talking for a while, her eyes repeatedly wandering to her enemy, Lady Tiernay. Presently Mr. Brummell entered the saloon and, catching sight of Eleanor, said affably,

"I believe this is my dance, Miss Sherburn?"

She rose, fluttering a smile at the Dowager.

"Enjoy yourself, my dear!" The Duchess's voice was slightly raised; glancing over to the corner Eleanor saw a scowl cross Lady Tiernay's face. Plainly she was seething at this attention which Eleanor was receiving from Society's leading notables.

"You are looking very beautiful tonight," Mr. Brummell was saying some time later when he and Eleanor, having danced together, were sitting out on a sofa at one end of the ballroom.

"Thank you, sir," she returned sedately, delicately fanning her cheeks. "It's kind of you to say so."

He smiled at the cool calm manner in which she received

his flattery. He, like the Marquis, was more used to females who simpered and blushed and averted their faces in a gesture of maidenly shyness.

"You're obviously not susceptible to flattery, Miss Sherburn," he commented.

"Oh, but make no mistake, sir! I have to own that it affords me a great deal of pleasure."

He laughed and for a moment fell silent. Eleanor looked at him, noting that there was nothing ostentatious about his clothes, yet they were of the most distinctive cut and colour. Their fit was flawless, and his cravat was perfection. Of medium height, with brown hair and humorous grey eyes, he had surprised Eleanor on her being presented to him; she had expected someone quite outstanding . . . like the Marquis.

However, there was a sort of drollery about Mr. Brummell that was excessively pleasing, an unassuming quietness that could not fail to appeal to a girl like Eleanor who had been brought up in the tranquil atmosphere of the country where people lived quietly and unobtrusively, not desiring to set fashions or become leaders of Society. It had amazed her, in fact, that such a man as Beau Brummell had managed to raise himself to his present position.

"You are a great success," he told her at length. "You've certainly made a creditable presentation."

"But then, sir, just look who was my patron."

"Prettily said. The Duchess has obviously endeared herself to you already."

"Indeed she has, sir! I owe her everything!"

"Everything?"

"Well . . . this success," said Eleanor.

"You'll owe her more when you make that brilliant match – "

"No!" she broke in swiftly. "That's impossible, sir." She was disconcerted, for the truth had almost slipped out –

that her expectations were so small as to be almost negligible. But just in time she remembered the Marquis's warning.

Mr. Brummell smiled faintly.

"You do realize, Miss Sherburn, that, having held both the Marquis and myself in conversation for no mean length of time, you are sure to become the rage?"

"But – how absurd!" she flashed, and this was out before she had time to draw it back.

"Absurd it might be," he agreed with a deepening of his smile, "but it is a fact, nevertheless."

"I'm sorry," she murmured faintly colouring. "I did not mean to slight you, sir."

"Nor did I take it as a slight, Miss Sherburn." His intelligent grey eyes rested on her and the curve of a smile still hovered upon his lips. "Haven't I just agreed with you over the absurdity that anyone should sway Society in this way?"

"Yes, sir, you have – and I admire you for the admission."

"I'm gratified to have earned your admiration, Miss Sherburn," he said in rather dry tones.

"I'm afraid, sir, that I do not curb my tongue as I should. If I have offended you by my lack of finesse then I pray your forgiveness."

To her surprise Mr. Brummell laughed.

"Do you know, Miss Sherburn, you're quite refreshing! I can understand why the Duchess took a liking to you."

Eleanor looked straight into his eyes, wondering if he had any inkling of the plot that was afoot. She decided he was in total ignorance of it, but felt sure that his friend the Marquis would eventually enlighten him.

"I doubt whether my Papa would describe my conduct as refreshing," she had to admit. "Rather would he admonish me for my tactlessness."

"Can I give you a word of advice, Miss Sherburn?"

"But of course. I shall welcome it, Mr. Brummell."

"Never admit to having made a mistake, be that mistake a slip of the tongue, an unconsidered act, or even a breach of etiquette." His grey eyes smiled ruefully. "It may surprise you to learn that I have reached my present position by following that rule."

"Really?" She looked puzzled, and yet a little contemptuous also. "So people say that the great Beau Brummell cannot make a mistake, I suppose?"

"If by 'people' you mean Fashionable Society, then the answer's yes, Miss Sherburn."

"But you are a friend of the Regent. Surely, if you were to commit some breach of etiquette when in his company you would have to make him an apology?"

Mr. Brummell shook his head emphatically.

"Not even to the Regent would I apologise. Nor would the Marquis – who is also a friend of the Regent."

"It seems very odd to me, sir. My Papa has always insisted that we apologise if we do anything wrong."

"And I am sure your Papa is right," he said after a pause. "While I, I'm afraid, am leading you astray."

She had to laugh then.

"No such thing, sir, for I would think for myself anyway."

"I believe you would," he murmured, and yet he went on to add, "However, my dear Miss Sherburn, there really are times when one should guard – at all costs – against lowering one's dignity."

"I shall remember that, sir," she smiled, aware suddenly of a pair of eyes fixed angrily upon her. She turned her head slightly ... to meet the gaze of Lady Tiernay.

CHAPTER
FOUR

As it happened, it was not to be very long before Eleanor was to recall the Beau's advice – and require to use it.

Having been invited to stand up with the handsome Earl of Brockheath, she had been brought – after the dance – to a small withdrawing-room where she and the Earl partook of some refreshment. The Earl, although a rather shy young man, had nevertheless complimented Eleanor on her appearance – on her gown and on the pretty manner in which her hair had been dressed. It was an altogether new and delightful fashion, he said. Perhaps it had been designed especially for brunettes?

"My hairdresser is a genius," returned Eleanor demurely, but at the same time congratulating herself on saying something which, could she have heard it, would have delighted the Duchess. "She did design this novel style exclusively for me." She glanced up as a shadow fell before her ... and looked into the lined and sallow face of Lady Tiernay.

The Earl instantly rose to his feet, making a bow.

"I thought I would like to chat with you, my dear," her ladyship purred smilingly, her eyes looking straight into Eleanor's.

Completely taken aback by this unexpected approach of her protectress's enemy, Eleanor could find nothing to say except,

"Oh – er – yes, ma'am," and rose to her feet.

The Earl, excusing himself, disappeared in the direction

of the ballroom. Lady Tiernay graciously requested Eleanor to be seated, while she herself took possession of a chair opposite to her.

"Firstly, Miss Sherburn, might I congratulate you on your charming appearance?"

"Thank you, ma'am."

"You have made quite a hit – but then you must be aware of the fact?"

"I'm told by Mr. Brummell that my presentation has been creditable," Eleanor could not help saying, again convinced that the Duchess would applaud this.

The woman facing her seemed to draw in her breath in a sort of hissing sound. However, the smile still hovered on the thin hard lips as, nodding her head, she said that such a comment from the great Mr. Brummell was something to be treasured.

"You are from Yorkshire, I'm told?"

"That's correct, ma'am."

"Er – your family? I take it that you are an heiress?"

Eleanor stiffened; it was here that the Beau's advice was recollected. She must guard against lowering her dignity . . . but how was this to be done without telling an untruth? – and this was quite unthinkable in a Vicar's daughter. There seemed to be only one way out of her dilemma, and although it might give the impression of rudeness, Eleanor decided that this could not be helped.

"I never discuss my personal affairs with strangers, ma'am."

Her companion's eyes glittered, and a flush of anger rose in her painted cheeks.

"Miss Sherburn," she snapped, "I was not probing into your personal affairs!"

"Then please forgive me, ma'am. I must have misunderstood you."

Silence, profound and most uncomfortable. It was

broken at last by Lady Tiernay, who had obviously decided that she ought not to have lost her temper.

"Perhaps, my dear, it is I who should apologise. It was not that I was portraying any sort of idle curiosity about your situation, but merely that I was anxious to show an interest in you."

"That is most kind in you, ma'am," returned Eleanor, fully aware that she was by no means out of the wood yet. There was the sort of expression on her companion's face that convinced Eleanor of her intention to learn more about the girl from Yorkshire who, even now, was the object of discussion by many of the men of fashion present at the ball. And no one could have failed to note the numerous glances of admiration that had repeatedly been cast in Eleanor's direction throughout the evening. Eleanor supposed the climax – as far as Lady Tiernay was concerned – was when the Earl of Brockheath – whom everyone considered as Isobel's beau – had approached Eleanor to stand up with him and then, at the end of the dance, had brought her here to partake of refreshments with him.

"Not at all, my dear Miss Sherburn. You see, I myself have brought out so many young females that I am naturally interested in the Dowager's two protégées. You are both so very attractive, in your different ways. Of course, you must know that blondes are the fashion – so silly, really," continued her ladyship with a hint of impatience that was clearly assumed, "but there it is. Had brunettes been in, then undoubtedly you would have been all the rage. Such a pity – but I expect you are resigned, my dear?"

Flushed with rising anger, Eleanor had once again to recall Mr. Brummell's advice. For without a doubt she was ready to say something cutting to her ladyship – thereby lowering her dignity.

"Who," she asked in tones of chill civility, "decrees what colour a girl's hair must be before she can become popular?"

Lady Tiernay shrugged her shoulders.

"It just happens, my dear. But, rather disastrous for you, blondes are *in* at the present time."

"They are?" said a cool and faintly amused voice from a spot by the door. "Your surprise me, my lady. Haven't you heard that the fashion is to undergo a dramatic and unexpected reversal, and that the brunette is to top the fashion?" The Marquis, flicking an imaginary speck of dust from his coat, moved with a sort of languid grace towards a vacant chair at Eleanor's elbow. "May I join you?" he enquired, slanting an amused glance at Eleanor. She found herself responding, and returned his smile. It savoured of a conspiracy, she thought, having been alerted at once to the fact that his lordship, upon overhearing some of the conversation between Lady Tiernay and herself, had decided to come to the rescue of his aunt's protégée. At his question, Lady Tiernay had turned pale, and her eyes had settled, with the most odd expression, on Eleanor's beautiful dark hair. Her ladyship began to nod her head, and with her quick insight Eleanor knew for sure that this woman had suddenly guessed what her old enemy was about.

"I'm just leaving." Her voice had a guttural sound, as if she were consumed by fury but was endeavouring to suppress it. Before she could rise the Marquis gallantly requested her to remain.

"It's such an age since you and I spoke together," he added quietly. "How is your charming granddaughter keeping? If appearances are anything to go by she is in the very pink of health."

"Isobel is well, thank you, my lord," returned her ladyship stiffly. "I saw that you stood up with her earlier."

"And most pleasant it was," suavely and yet, decided Eleanor, sincerely also. "The Lady Isobel is noted for her lightness in the waltz."

"It is gallant of you to remark upon it, my lord."

"Not at all, ma'am." His dark blue eyes flickered towards Eleanor. "I expect you have high hopes of your granddaughter's future being settled before very long?" The Marquis's tones were faintly bored, Eleanor noticed, yet in his eyes that hint of amusement could still be plainly discerned.

"As you must have noticed, my lord, the Earl of Brockheath is more than a little interested in her."

How indelicate of her ladyship to say a thing like that, thought Eleanor – and she saw by the changed expression in the Marquis's eyes that he was thinking the same thing. But it was as if Lady Tiernay just had to convince both the Marquis and Eleanor herself that her granddaughter was still the Incomparable, still the star of this Season's debutantes.

"I felicitate you," murmured his lordship softly. "The Lady Isobel could do no better than marry the heir to the Dukedom."

"Her expectations are enormous, her only brother having perished at sea – but I expect you know about it?"

The Marquis said nothing; he was looking at Eleanor, taking in the delicate colour of her cheeks, the pointed little chin, the generous mouth. His eyes wandered to her shoulders, then to her hair. Faintly he smiled, as if at some private joke. Eleanor suspected he was thinking about his aunt, and her intention of changing the fashion. Without being aware of it she lifted a hand to finger one of her ringlets, while with the other hand she daintily moved the fan, keeping it well below her eyes. She had no idea just how lovely she looked, or that the Marquis, used even as he was to beautiful women, was – not without experiencing some considerable surprise – finding the picture most arresting indeed. She met his stare, lowered her long curling lashes, for his eyes were too disconcerting by far, and at the same time wondered what this new experience was – this inexplicable fluttering of a pulse ...

Lady Tiernay was rising from her chair; the Marquis rose also, and stood until she had passed from sight through the open door. Then he turned, to look down from his great height into the expressive brown eyes of the young lady sitting there, her painted fan idle in her hand now, but her fingers still playing with the tip of one long black ringlet.

"Thank you, my lord," she said simply.

"It was nothing. My aunt would have wished me to rescue you."

"I was rather scared that she would ask me more awkward questions. It was such a relief to hear your voice."

"*More* awkward questions?" The Marquis looked interrogatingly at her. "So I wasn't really in time?"

"She wanted to know about my situation."

The dark blue eyes narrowed.

"You didn't enlighten her, I hope?"

"No, sir. You see, Mr. Brummell had advised me never to lower my dignity. I remembered his advice, and followed it."

"He'll be gratified," returned the Marquis smoothly. "Tell me," he invited, taking possession of the chair which her ladyship had just vacated, and which was opposite Eleanor, rather than beside her, where he had previously been seated, "what were the questions she asked you?"

"She wanted to know if I was an heiress."

"She asked you that outright?"

"Yes, my lord, she did."

"Deplorable. She must be greatly troubled to forget her manners like that."

"Troubled?" inquired Eleanor, suddenly remembering that, as she was not supposed to know what was going on, she would be expected to evince some degree of curiosity. "What would her ladyship be troubled about?"

"It need not cause you any anxiety," was the Marquis's rather abrupt answer. "I presume you did not oblige her ladyship by answering her question?"

"No, sir," returned Eleanor firmly, "I did not."

His lordship looked curiously at her; she saw his eyes examining her face ... and wondered if she were mistaken, or whether that really was a hint of admiration she perceived lurking in their depths.

"By what clever prevarication did you evade doing so?"

"I'm afraid I was rude, my lord."

His eyebrows shot up.

"You were, Miss Sherburn?"

She nodded her head, aware of the hint of colour that was creeping into her cheeks.

"I told her I never discussed my personal affairs with strangers."

A small silence ensued and then, smiling, the Marquis said,

"Her Grace will applaud that when she hears of it."

"She will?" innocently as Eleanor once again remembered to evince curiosity.

"My aunt has little time for Lady Tiernay," was all he said, then immediately changed the subject. "Your cousin, Miss Doynsby – she appears to have got over her fit of the doldrums, I noticed just now. She was enjoying the company of the Duke of Elveton, who had led her into a set of quadrilles."

"She was?" breathed Eleanor, her brown eyes widening. "Oh, but this is famous news you bring me, sir!"

"You appear most concerned about your cousin?"

"Yes, indeed. It was such a shame that she was pining for her Hugh ..." Eleanor's voice trailed off as she noticed the sudden quivering of her companion's mouth. "I expect it sounds amusing to you, sir," she said severely, "but I assure you it is the most serious thing! Beatrix's Mama has always set her heart upon her daughter marrying well."

His lordship's eyes became fixed on Eleanor's face again.

"And you ... has not your Mama the same ambition for you?"

Eleanor shook her head.

"It isn't possible for me to do so," she said resignedly.

"No? Why?

She looked at him with a rather startled expression.

"Surely your aunt has enlightened you as to my situation, sir?"

The Marquis took out a diamond-studded snuff-box and held it in his hand for a moment before flicking back the lid.

"It is most unfashionable to mention one's poverty," he said sternly at last. "You keep such things to yourself."

"But I did – when speaking to Lady Tiernay. But with you, sir, I can be frank, seeing that your aunt will surely have mentioned my situation to you. In any case, you know that my Papa is only a parson and, therefore, I must be poor, mustn't I?"

He frowned on hearing the word poor.

"I advise you to forget your poverty while you are here." His lordship took a pinch of snuff and put it to his nose. It was Eleanor's turn to frown now, since the action was excessively distasteful to her. The Marquis, on noting her expression, stopped in the act of closing the lid of the box, and lifted his straight black brows in a gesture of arrogant inquiry. As she remained silent he asked her why she was frowning.

"It's nothing," she murmured, but his lordship was insistent.

"You don't frown for nothing," he pointed out. And when she refused to comment he added, in tones of cold civility, "You object to snuff, it would appear?"

Eleanor swallowed hard, aware that she and the Marquis

seemed always to have dissension creep into their conversation.

"I have no right to object," she said meekly.

"But you do, nevertheless?"

She had to be honest with him and say yes, she did object.

"I think it's – well – a foppish habit," she added, peeping at him from beneath her lashes. His face was an inscrutable mask.

"A habit adopted by Dandies, in fact?" His lordship's voice was crisp.

"I must try to curb my tongue," she began when the Marquis interrupted her.

"It was your *expression*, ma'am!"

She bit her lip.

"I beg your pardon, sir."

Before he could make any further retort another couple entered the saloon, and on seeing who the girl was Eleanor uttered a little exclamation of pleasure.

"Beatrix! Are you enjoying yourself, after all?"

Beatrix, having left the side of the gentleman who had escorted her into the saloon, and who was now obtaining a glass of orgeat for her, came towards her cousin with a faint smile upon her lips.

"Yes, indeed, Eleanor. And you?" Beatrix's eyes moved, to settle on the Marquis's handsome face, and he it was who replied to her question – whether from sarcasm or because he really believed the query was addressed to him, Eleanor could not quite determine. However, having learned a little about the character of my lord, she rather thought it was the former, since she had herself experienced his sarcasm on more than one occasion.

"Tolerably well, thank you, Miss Doynsby. Your cousin's company during the past few moments has been pleasantly diverting." Having risen, he offered Beatrix his chair.

Eleanor looked uncertainly at him; as before, his face was an unreadable mask.

"Thank you, sir." Beatrix sat down, and looked up at his lordship, a sweet smile fluttering on her pretty mouth. A golden maiden, thought Eleanor appreciatively. It was no wonder she had been the rage at the assemblies she and Eleanor had attended in York. She would probably be the rage here, also, despite the fact that the Duchess was planning to reduce the popularity of blondes. "I agree that my dear cousin's company can be diverting."

A small silence followed. Eleanor wondered if his lordship was waiting for some evidence of the coldness about which Eleanor had warned him. It would appear that Beatrix had changed her mind about setting this Leader of Fashion against her, for she was smiling up at him still, and in the most alluring manner possible. Watching his face, and the movement of a muscle in the hardness of his jaw, Eleanor saw that – perhaps against his will – he was beginning to be affected by the pale golden beauty of her cousin. If Beatrix could manage to engage the affections of the Marquis ... what a triumph it would be! True, he was a confirmed bachelor, but even confirmed bachelors had been known to succumb to beauty less ravishing than that possessed by Beatrix.

The young Duke of Elveton returned, handed Beatrix her drink, then turned to the Marquis and said,

"Justin, will you be kind enough to give me your valuable opinion of this coat of mine? I had it from Crighton – the tailor they say is going to oust all the others, his cut and style being impeccable!"

His lordship, who could not help but notice the contempt that had crept into Miss Sherburn's brown eyes, stared her down for a long and disconcerting moment until, unable to hold that piercing gaze a second longer, she fluttered her lashes and lowered her eyes.

Turning his attention to the Duke's coat at last, his lordship examined it with what appeared to be the utmost care ... and yet, for some reason she could not define, Eleanor gained the firm impression that his interest was nothing more than cursory.

"Who did you say made it?" enquired his lordship at last.

"Crighton ..." The young Duke was clearly on tenter-hooks as he awaited the Nonpareil's verdict. Eleanor could almost hear his relieved indrawing of a breath when presently the Marquis said, "He'll go far, Richard. I congratulate you on discovering him."

"Justin – I'm greatly in your debt! My friend, John Ormond, swore you would deplore the material. Wait until I tell him of your approval!" Clearly the Duke was de-lighted; Eleanor, again catching the Marquis's eye, could not possibly miss his amused expression. A smile broke, and his humour was infectious. She was suppressing laugh-ter now, and she knew for sure that the Marquis was fully aware of this.

"What a perfectly charming snuff-box!" exclaimed Beatrix suddenly. "Please, my lord, might I look more closely at it?"

"But of course, Miss Doynsby." The box was handed over; Beatrix went into raptures over the exquisite work-manship.

"Prinny gave it to you?" The Duke spoke carelessly, just as if the giving away of diamond-studded snuff-boxes was an everyday occurrence. "I received a similar one from him, when I attended a dinner party at Carlton House last month."

"I recall his giving away several of these," remarked his lordship. "I was not at that particular dinner, being away on family business."

"Does the Prince Regent often present such lavish gifts?" Eleanor could not resist enquiring. Her Papa's stipend for a whole year would not buy even one snuff-box of this quality.

"The Regent is the most generous of men," declared the Duke loyally. "We who are his friends are among the most fortunate people in the country. What say you, Justin?"

The Marquis did not say anything. Aware that he was being closely watched by Miss Sherburn, he turned a wide and arrogant stare upon her. She was tempted to point out that any gifts the Regent might dole out to his cronies in the raffish Carlton House Set, came from the toil of the common people, by whose endeavours his ostentatious and deplorably extravagant style of living was made possible. However, mindful of the fact that his lordship belonged to the Carlton House Set, and mindful also that she must not earn his dislike, she maintained a prudent silence.

"Your snuff-box," said Beatrix, handing it back. "It is very beautiful, sir."

Eleanor, having turned away, began idly to fan herself, wondering why she felt such a strange element of disappointment that the Marquis was one of the Dandy Set, taking snuff, giving too much time to frivolities, being foppishly concerned with his clothes. But at least, compared with some of the other Corinthians present, he did not wear jewellery. Nothing, in her eyes, could be more effeminate than the diamond pin the Duke was wearing in his cravat.

Beatrix, however, was later to express somewhat unexpected enthusiasm regarding the Duke.

"Isn't he good-looking, Eleanor! I felt quite the thing when he paid me so much attention! He led me into the quadrilles, and then we waltzed! It was so enjoyable – you have no idea!"

"I'm relieved that you are taking an interest in your ball, Beatrix. You had me greatly troubled earlier, when you were crying."

"My ball," said Beatrix, ignoring the rest of what her cousin had said. "This ball is for both of us, dearest Eleanor!"

Her cousin said nothing to this, but recalled with a secret grimace that Beatrix had been quite pettish earlier in the evening, complaining that all this was supposed to be for her. However, so pleased was she that Beatrix had lifted herself out of the doldrums, Eleanor did not think of bringing up anything like that. Instead, she said how much she herself was enjoying the ball, remembering to thank Beatrix for wanting her to come to London as her companion.

"If it hadn't been for you," she added, giving her cousin's arm an affectionate squeeze, "I should never have had an experience like this. I shall remember it all my life!"

"There isn't any need for gratitude," Beatrix told her. "I myself would not have been here if you had refused to accompany me."

"And you're really glad that you're here?"

Beatrix glanced over to where the Duke was standing, chatting with two other elegant gentlemen. After a second, her eyes moved to the Marquis, standing so tall and straight and aristocratic, talking to his aunt.

"Yes," replied Beatrix with a soulful sigh, "I most certainly am glad that I'm here."

Following the direction of her eyes, Eleanor murmured, "What do you think of the Marquis?"

"He's all you said – and more! What a noble bearing! And have you ever seen anyone quite so handsome? He's manly, too, don't you think?"

"Manly?" frowned Eleanor thinking of the diamond-studded snuff-box. "Do you know, Beatrix, I find that few gentlemen of the ton are manly."

Beatrix blinked at this pronouncement.

"How can you say so? Lord Trouvaine is certainly manly, as is the Duke of Elveton." She paused, offering her cousin an opportunity of saying something, but Eleanor merely gave a slight shrug of her shoulders, denoting her disagreement. "I can't think how you have come to regard the Marquis as effeminate," said Beatrix in tones of indignation.

"I didn't say he was effeminate, Beatrix, only that I dislike intensely the jewelled snuff-box – "

"But all gentlemen of the ton have them. It was a present from the Prince Regent himself – you heard him say so."

"The Duke said so," corrected Eleanor. "However, I expect the Regent did hand it out, along with many others. In any case, it matters not from where Lord Trouvaine obtained it; it's the fact of his using it that brands him foppish in my estimation."

"It's only because of your Papa," decided Beatrix after some thought. "He would not approve of anything we have here, I'm sure."

"He would like the Duchess."

"My aunt's attitude towards you is most puzzling to me, Eleanor. She treats you like a daughter."

Eleanor nodded, conscious that her cousin's eyes were travelling over the beautiful ball gown which the Duchess had bought for her.

"I must agree that she has taken an extraordinary liking to me." Eleanor looked anxiously at her cousin. "You are not annoyed, Beatrix?"

"No, of course not, dearest Eleanor! I am glad for you that my aunt is making your sojourn here so memorable."

At this Eleanor was able to relax. It would have caused her some considerable heartache were Beatrix to resent the interest which the Duchess was taking in her. She would very much have liked to confide in Beatrix, repeating what she had overheard, which explained that, as a matter of fact, she *was* being treated like a daughter, simply because of her resemblance to that unfortunate young lady. However, as she could not confide in her cousin, she changed the subject, returning, quite automatically, to the Marquis.

"He has spent some time with us both, and so we are made," she said happily. "Your aunt says we shall be showered with invitations."

"Yes, I know. Oh, how did you like Lady Jersey? I own she's handsome, but I found her arrogant and sort of – of malicious when she was talking about some unfortunate young lady who, having displeased her, was refused a voucher for Almack's."

"I must admit I found her rather overpowering," admitted Eleanor. "I think it was because I knew I dared not offend her in any way; that, on the contrary, I had to adopt a meek and almost servile manner with her, just so that I would be favoured with a voucher. She's promised to send me one, as I expect she has you?"

"Yes." Beatrix moved closer to her cousin and whispered in her ear, "I heard someone say that she and the Regent have been philandering for some time."

Eleanor said nothing. She was of the opinion that the Regent spent much of his time philandering. A man of his position who openly admitted that his tailor and his bookmaker were of more importance than his politics was, in her eyes, quite beyond the pale. She found herself wishing that the Marquis was not his friend, that he despised the future king just as much as she herself did – and as much as Papa would, thought Eleanor, recalling how often he preached against indulging in the good things of this life.

It was much later when, having danced until the early hours of the morning, Eleanor and Beatrix decided to find a quiet spot and indulge in another tête-á-tête, where they happened to overhear the Duchess and her nephew talking. They were sitting on the other side of the couch occupied by the cousins, and as the back was exceptionally high, Eleanor and Beatrix had not noticed that they were there.

"She'll be the rage, no doubt about it."

"I agree. Your little provincial's face has glowed as I'm sure it has never glowed before. Can't you imagine her, when she gets back to her country parsonage, boring everyone she meets with a highly-coloured account of her brilliant London debut?" A laugh escaped the Marquis, while as for Eleanor – her cheeks were burning, her small hand tightly clenched upon her fan. Within her, anger flared; she felt at this moment that she must forget all her Papa's teaching and allow bitter hatred to enter into her heart.

"Dearest Eleanor," said Beatrix in a very low tone, "he doesn't mean you."

"He mentioned the parsonage." Eleanor's voice was choked. "Besides, I've heard him refer to me as the provincial before."

"I don't know what to say," began Beatrix, much distressed.

"Then don't say anything – please!"

But this was ignored as her cousin continued,

"How perfectly odious of him! And to think that I championed him when you branded him a fop! How can he say such horrid things about you? Why, you're never bored anyone in the whole of your life!"

White now, and trembling, Eleanor would have liked to move away, to walk in front of his lordship, just to let him know that he had been overheard. But of course she remained where she was, and heard the Duchess admonish her nephew severely and then add,

"She's a dear sweet child, Justin, but you – oh, you are such a cynic where women are concerned. If you left the opera-dancers alone you might have time to learn about ordinary women. However, that is another matter. What I am concerned with at the present time is making her the rage and so I hope, in spite of your opinion of the child, you will do as I ask and let her be seen *regularly* in your company?"

Eleanor shot a glance at her cousin. To her utter relief and amazement Beatrix immediately said, a frown upon her wide forehead,

"What did my aunt say? I couldn't catch it."

Breathing a deep sigh, Eleanor shook her head in a gesture of resignation and replied that it was nothing of importance.

The Marquis was speaking, but very softly, and once again Eleanor realised from her expression that Beatrix could not hear.

"Do not worry, my dear aunt. I'll see that the chit is seen in my company – and perhaps we shall begin tomorrow by riding in the Park."

CHAPTER
FIVE

THAT Eleanor had taken the Polite World by storm was soon evident; for days after the ball invitations poured in, invitations which included both girls, but Beatrix, displaying rather more intelligence than usual, declared at once that the "star" attraction was Eleanor.

"It's the oddest thing," she muttered with slight peevishness, "but whereas in York *I* was the rage – the one always sought after – here it is *you*."

Flushing slightly, Eleanor murmured something about its being only a temporary thing, and that it was the white Valenciennes lace ball gown which had made her outstanding, for undoubtedly it was one of the most attractive gowns to be seen.

"No, Eleanor," argued Beatrix, shaking her head so that her pretty golden ringlets swayed and moved in the most enchanting manner, "it's you yourself. I had not before noticed that you are really beautiful, and I suppose this omission occurred as a result of Mama's persistent assertions that you were always cast in the shade by me."

"But I *was* cast in the shade," Eleanor could not help reminding her. "At the assemblies in York it was always you who were sought after."

Beatrix looked at her in a very thoughtful way.

"I have been pondering that circumstance, Eleanor, and I have come to the conclusion that all those gentlemen who hung around me were interested in my expectations."

"But, no," protested Eleanor. "What makes you say a think like that?"

"Because there, they all knew that I am an heiress, and that my income will one day be nine thousand a year. Here, people are not aware of our different situations; they probably conclude that we are both heiresses."

Eleanor had nothing to say to this. She herself had reached the conclusion that, dressing as she did, and wearing one of the most beautiful diamonds to be seen at the ball, and having as her patron the exalted Dowager Duchess of Carandale, it must appear to everyone that she was a Somebody. Later, she was convinced, they would learn the truth – that the Duchess had foisted upon them a provincial Nobody. This was the old lady's method of revenge for the untimely death of her lovely daughter.

True to his word, the Marquis had called at his aunt's house in Cavendish Square on the day following the ball, and had taken Eleanor driving in Hyde Park where, during this fashionable hour, his lordship was hailed many times by his friends and acquaintances. Eleanor, with his derogatory words still ringing in her ears, had scarcely been able to afford him civility. However, on thinking over the situation into which she had been propelled as a result of her Grace's desire for revenge, she decided that her most sensible course would be to forget what she had heard and adopt towards the Marquis a sort of light-hearted complacency, accepting his compliments with a casualness that would leave him in no doubt whatsoever that she valued his flattery not at all. This should put him in his place, since, owing to the position he occupied in London Society as a notable Corinthian, a veritable Nonpareil and Leader of Fashion, it was to be presumed that those young females upon whom he deigned to bestow his attention would always be thrown into confusion by his compliments. And so, accordingly, Eleanor accepted all he had to say with a dignified inclination of her head, or a smile that could only be described as faintly condescending. That his lordship was piqued was made plain more than once during that first drive in the Park, and when he had eventually driven her back to Cavendish Square he had become quite coldly silent. Nevertheless, he called the next day, and the one after that, so it became a familiar sight for those Fashionables who frequented Hyde Park to see her up beside his lordship, dressed in the very crack of fashion, her black curls gleaming in the sunshine.

"The Marquis has certainly become interested in you," declared Beatrix, when, on Eleanor's return from one of her drives, she and her cousin sat together in the drawing-room of her Grace's home. "It's rather a risk for you to encourage him, don't you think?" went on Beatrix, looking anxiously at Eleanor. "He will not be interested in you once he knows of your situation."

Eleanor turned to face her.

"You're forgetting, Beatrix, what your aunt said about Lord Trouvaine. He is a confirmed bachelor. But in any case, as he can have his pick of the beautiful daughters of the nobility, he would scarcely choose a Nobody like me."

Beatrix appeared to be troubled still.

"Do you think, then, that he is flirting with you?"

Eleanor hesitated, fervently wishing she could set her cousin's mind at rest by divulging all she knew, by telling her that the Marquis was showing interest in her solely because he desired to please his aunt.

"He could be flirting with me," replied Eleanor guardedly.

"Then, my dearest Eleanor, you must be careful not to take him seriously."

Eleanor had to smile.

"You forget that he said the most odious things about me."

"Yes, I know he did, but I now believe he has changed his mind about you."

"If he is flirting then he hasn't changed his mind about me," was Eleanor's perfectly logical rejoinder.

"I believe I'm becoming muddled about his lordship," said Beatrix impatiently. "He acts in the oddest manner, first of all saying the most unkind things about you and since then coming every day to take you driving in Hyde Park. It doesn't make sense to me."

"Don't worry your head about it, Beatrix. Instead, tell me about his Grace the Duke of Elveton? *He* has taken *you* driving, remember."

Beatrix's eyes shone at the mention of the Duke.

"It is doing me no end of good to be seen with him! All the notable whips hail him, and he told me today that he is a member of the Four-in-Hand Club."

"Is that something special?" inquired Eleanor without much interest.

"Only the very cream can join," answered Beatrix, her eyes widening at the idea of her cousin's ignorance. "I do not know if the Marquis is a member, but I should think it very likely."

Eleanor hesitated before voicing her next question.

"Leaving aside the fact that being seen in the Duke's company is doing you good socially, how do you feel about him?"

"You mean – have I a *tendre* for him? No ... I don't think so ..."

Eleanor smiled.

"You are not sure?"

"I do not suppose so exalted a man would choose me for his wife." Beatrix's expression became dreamy. She said, after a rather long and undecided pause, "Do you know, Eleanor, I am fast admitting that it would not have done at all for me to have married Hugh."

A sigh of relief escaped Eleanor. Although she had suspected that her cousin had begun to forget her farmer beau, she had not been absolutely sure.

"I'm glad that you have reached that decision, Beatrix."

Her cousin nodded thoughtfully.

"I'm not cut out for hard work," she rejoined with a rather self-deprecating smile.

"I did think," murmured Eleanor after a pause, "that it would be a triumph for you to succeed in turning the Marquis away from his determination to retain his bachelor state."

"You mean – manage to gain his interest?" Again Beatrix's blue eyes shone. "He is handsome, and popular! I must say, dear cousin, that I would like it above all things if I were to be a regular guest at Carlton House! – and this I would be were I to marry Lord Trouvaine, who is one of the Set!"

However, Lord Trouvaine's interest at present lay wholly with Eleanor, and Beatrix made no move to divert it to herself. He continued to drive Eleanor round the Park in his curricle, alternating between stiff and dignified silences and attempts to send his enchanting companion into confusion either by paying her compliments or, when this failed, by treating her to his cutting sarcasm or arrogant satire. She resisted all his efforts, hiding her dislike; but sometimes, his odious words caused her so deep a sense of humiliation that she could scarcely bring herself to answer any question he might put to her.

One day, while driving in the Park, he turned to her and inquired if she were feeling quite well.

"Of course," she answered in some surprise. "Why do you ask, sir?"

"You're more than ordinarily quiet today." His tones were crisp and cold. "I thought perhaps your recent late nights had begun to tell upon you."

"What an indiscreet thing to say!" she could not help exclaiming. "Are you implying, my lord, that I look jaded?"

"So it *is* possible to arouse some emotion in you," was his satirical rejoinder. "You look rather charming when in a fury, Miss Sherburn."

She did not blush, as he had hoped. Instead, she ignored the compliment and returned to the subject of her general appearance.

"You failed to answer my question, sir. I asked if I looked jaded?"

The Marquis did not reply for a space; he was acknowledging the greetings of a friend who, with his latest bit of muslin sitting prettily in the seat beside him, was driving a pair of lively greys.

"I daresay you are well aware, Miss Sherburn, that you are not looking jaded." His lordship turned his head. She noted with extreme satisfaction that he was having difficulty in curbing his rising temper.

And because she could not resist irritating him further she found herself saying, in cool and haughty tones, "Then why, my lord, did you *imply* that I was looking jaded?"

He almost dropped the reins in astonishment. No female had ever dared go that far with him before! Eleanor did not know it, but his lordship had the greatest difficulty in refraining from setting her down, right in the middle of the Park, and telling her to walk home.

"I'm afraid, ma'am," he said icily, "that your northern manners leave much to be desired!"

She did blush then, and was furious that he should turn his head at that moment. The light of cold triumph in his eyes did nothing to ease her embarrassment.

"Perhaps I should apologise," she ventured presently, thinking of the Duchess and fearing her displeasure if the Marquis should decide to wash his hands of her protégée.

"Perhaps?" repeated his lordship with an arrogant lift of his brows. "Ma'am, do not trouble to apologise unless you are sure you owe me an apology."

She bit her lip, nervously fingering her reticule. She knew she had gone too far this time – but how was she to extricate herself? That he was puzzled was of course understandable, as it must appear to him that her antagonism was without cause. It was a pity she could not turn to him and say,

"Twice, my lord, I have overheard you saying the most odious and unkind things about me." However, as this was not possible she continued to try to think of some way of appeasing him without causing herself too much discomfiture. In the end she had to admit that an apology was the only course open to her.

"I'm sorry, my lord," she said at last meekly.

"It puzzles me," he remarked some time later, "why you do not refuse to accompany me for these drives?"

Again she could have explained by telling him that she knew of his aunt's plan to make her the rage.

"I believe that to be seen in your company, my lord, will ensure my coming into fashion."

He seemed stunned by this open admission.

"You are the most forthright young lady I have ever met!" he said.

"My Papa, sir, taught me always to be honest."

His lordship looked at her with some suspicion.

"And did he also teach you to measure swords with all those people you dislike?"

Again she bit her lip, for this was plain speaking indeed. It was not ladylike for her to continue with this sparring, and yet, for some reason she could not for the life of her explain, she was driven on to do so.

"I am of the impression, my lord, that it is *you* who do not like *me*."

"I am compelled to give the lie to that, Miss Sherburn. Never, to my knowledge, have I displayed a dislike of you."

"It is an impression, sir."

"I cannot be held accountable for your impressions!"

She turned her face towards him; she could not help but notice that his dark eyes, although hard and angry, also revealed a hint of admiration in their depths. She recalled a strange unfathomable stirring of her emotions ... the reason being that she was passing through the same experience again.

"Is it wrong?" she queried, just because she had to. "Am I mistaken in believing that you dislike me?"

She felt a hypocrite, because in spite of his angry retort, she knew full well that he disliked her. He made no reply, and she realised that it was not possible for him to do so – unless he lied, of course.

A week later the two cousins paid their first visit to Almack's Assembly Rooms. Having driven out earlier that day with the Marquis, Eleanor had inquired politely if he would be there. His answer was evasive; he had not yet made up his mind, he said. Strangely, much as she disliked him, Eleanor had a subconscious desire to see him at this most exclusive club. The reason for this vague yet insistent wish continued to elude her.

The Dowager, having seen that both girls were dressed to perfection in the height of fashion, took them in her crested barouche, its high-stepping greys handled expertly by Skiffy, the Duchess's coachman, who had George the groom on the box beside him. For Eleanor, this driving in state was still a novelty, despite the fact that she had now done it on a number of occasions. She leant back against the luxurious upholstery and uttered a long, contented sigh. Her protectress looked at her from the seat opposite, and a smile of extreme satisfaction crossed her face. She was well on the way to success with her plan; already it was being accepted in Polite Circles that the brunette was to supplant the blonde in popularity. She, the Duchess, had taken both girls shopping in Bond Street on a number of occasions, buying for them both ... yet by some subtle manoeuvre Eleanor's hats and bonnets, her shoes and reticules, her pelisses and shawls, were all just that little bit more modish than those of Beatrix. Fortunately, as that young lady had an enormous amount of beautiful clothes and accessories to go with them, she did not even notice that a distinction was being made in favour of her cousin.

As for Eleanor's own feelings – she often knew a deep embarrassment at the money that was being expended upon her, yet she would inevitably come to the conclusion that, as there was nothing she could do about it, she might as well accept all these gifts with both resignation and pleasure. For there was no denying that she derived a great amount of pleasure from wearing such modish clothes, and the hats and bonnets which caused so many heads to turn whenever she was walking or riding, either with the Duchess or his lordship. Several other young gallants had sought to take her driving, including Mr. Brummell himself. And as the Duchess said she must accept one or two of these offers, Eleanor had by now been seen with no less than four Marquises and three Earls. The wealthy Mr. Frederick Tattersall had shown interest in her, being heard to say that he did not know why he had ever looked at a blonde. They had no character, he declared. Brunettes, now, did have character, and a beauty that would still be theirs when the blondes had become frowsy and grey-headed. All this was so nonsensical to Eleanor that she found herself laughing when the Marquis obviously expected her to be gratified by his comment.

"It just goes to prove how utterly absurd it all is! Doesn't a gentleman want anything except looks in his wife? Can't he see that what is beneath the surface is what really counts? Blondes ... brunettes! Fustian!"

The Marquis had laughed too, thoroughly enjoying her indignation – and, she strongly suspected, agreeing with all she was saying.

Strangely, Beatrix took no exception to all the adulation which was coming her cousin's way. She was now occupied in a flirtation with Lord Mauduit, but she also had dangling after her none other than the Marquis of Tutbury, heir to the Duke of Winnick. However, in the opinion of the Duchess, this attention was enjoyed by Beatrix solely because she was the cousin of Eleanor, although her Grace naturally did not say this in her niece's hearing. But, she maintained, all the notables were now attracted to brunettes, the Incomparable already having fallen from favour, her titled beau having developed a decided interest in the dark-haired girl from Yorkshire.

The assembly at Almack's was attended by many of the ton already known to Eleanor and Beatrix, and as they entered they were greeted by nods and smiles from almost everyone present. However, on catching the baleful eye of Lady Tiernay, Eleanor turned away swiftly, the woman's hatred seeming to eat right into her very soul. Her granddaughter, the Lady Isobel, was sitting with her, looking rather lost, and with a pout to her mouth and a scowling expression in her cornflower blue eyes.

Eleanor heard the long-drawn-out sigh of satisfaction uttered by the Duchess, and knew that her triumph was almost complete.

No less a personage than Mr. Brummell himself led Eleanor into the country dance. He had arrived early, which was remarkable since, like his friend the Marquis of Trouvaine, he was in the habit of arriving about a minute before eleven, the hour when the doors were firmly closed by the orders of the club's dreaded patronesses. This evening the patronesses present were Lady Jersey – who had sent the cousins the vouchers – and the formidable and imperious Mrs. Drummond Burrell.

After the country dance was over Eleanor was besieged by others wishing to dance with her. Flushed by her success, she at length retired to a small saloon to partake of refreshments, escorted by one of the Season's most eligible bachelors, Mr. Horace Cothele whose estates in Berkshire and Wiltshire were said to be enormous.

"Miss Sherburn, I really must congratulate you on that delightful gown. How well it tones with your lovely dark hair!"

She thanked him primly, aware that he made no exaggeration regarding her gown. Of beige satin trimmed with point-lace, it fitted her slender figure to perfection, being high-waisted, with pretty flouncing running all around the hem. Her curls, dressed this time in a style of enchanting simplicity, fell in a glorious shining mass on to her shoulders. From the waist hung a dainty reticule and from her wrist a painted fan hung from a beige silk ribbon.

Mr. Cothele later asked her to stand up with him for the waltz but, having been briefed by the Dowager about the impropriety of taking part in the dance until one of the patronesses had signalled her approval, Eleanor politely refused his invitation. The dance, still frowned upon by those whose ideas were old-fashioned, had been learned by both Eleanor and Beatrix at the local assemblies at home, and it was a most frustrating experience for them to be forced to sit there pretending to be unconcerned and watching other young ladies enjoying themselves.

"I feel like accepting the next gentleman who asks me," said Beatrix with a frown. "I hate sitting here like this!"

"You mustn't stand up," warned Eleanor. "Don't forget, the fact that we've been given vouchers doesn't mean that we're members for life. Your aunt stressed that, were we to do the least thing to displease any of the patronesses, we could be made to forfeit our vouchers."

This seemed to make an impression on Beatrix, for she refused two gentlemen afterwards. However, she did stand up in the end, with the Marquis of Avonlee who, it appeared, had first approached Lady Jersey.

It was to be Lord Trouvaine with whom Eleanor was destined to dance. Arriving at his normal hour of five minutes to eleven, he stood for a long moment, looking round the room, a bored expression on his lean and handsome face. Then his eyes alighted on Eleanor, sitting demurely at the Dowager's side. Smiling faintly to himself, he strolled over to where Lady Jersey was talking to a couple of other ladies. Eleanor, who had seen him enter, allowed her eyes to follow him, and to seek his face as he spoke to the patroness. Lady Jersey smiled, looked at Eleanor, then came towards her with the Marquis. A moment later Eleanor was swung into the waltz, her tiny waist encircled by his lordship's arm, while her right hand was taken firmly into his grasp. She felt the warmth of his other hand through her dress for a few seconds before he moved it away. The hand holding hers was strong and his fingers moved with a sort of gentle caress over the back of her hand. Suddenly she recalled her cousin's warning that his lordship might be indulging in a flirtation with her. Eleanor knew that her behaviour lately had piqued him more than ever, the reason being that not for a single moment did she display any emotion whatsoever in response to the many compliments he had paid to her. She had suspected him of deriving some measure of amusement from the encounters, had somehow known that he was endeavouring to break down her reserve. Defeat in his dealings with the opposite sex had been unknown to him until he met Eleanor; of this she had no doubt at all. No wonder that he was piqued, or that he refused to admit to defeat. His pride would suffer too much, he was thinking. Also, he was, she felt sure, still more than a little confident of scoring a victory over her. Well, he would see! The arrogant and self-opinionated Marquis of Trouvaine would have to admit, in the end, that he had met his match!

"You are very quiet, Miss Sherburn," he said, his mouth so close to her cheek that she could feel his warm breath upon it. His head was bent, and she knew that if she dared to lift her face it would undoubtedly touch his chin.

"I'm listening to the music, my lord."

"A pretty tune, is it not?" His voice was expressionless, yet she strongly suspected he was laughing at her.

"Most haunting, my lord."

"I myself find it exhilarating."

"I suppose that is not a bad description."

"You obviously learned the waltz at home?"

"Yes, we did -- at the York assemblies."

"What does Papa think about it?"

"He disapproves."

"So . . . you are acting against his wishes?"

She did look up then, for he had himself straightened to his full height. Her head reached only to his shoulder and suddenly she felt rather insignificant . . . and pleasantly helpless.

"Mama would not mind my standing up for the waltz," she said, unable to repress the dimple that peeped out as a smile fluttered to her mouth.

"You haven't answered my question, Miss Sherburn," he reminded her gently. "It was Papa of whom I was speaking."

"I'm not really acting against his wishes," she began, then stopped, a flush tinting her cheeks in the most beguiling way.

"So you can tell fibs on occasion, Miss Sherburn?"

"I do not understand what this cross-examination is all about my lord."

"I'm of the opinion that your Papa would be quite shocked if he knew what was happening to you," said his lordship unexpectedly.

"I write home regularly," she retorted.

"I'll wager you leave out more than you put in!"

"Why should I leave anything out, sir? I have done nothing of which I am ashamed!"

"Have you told your Papa that you are all the rage?"

"Well ... no. You see, he considers such things as frivolous."

"Like taking snuff, maybe?" he said with mocking satire.

Eleanor's colour heightened.

"I'm told that most gentlemen take snuff."

"But you still do not approve?"

"It's so unnecessary," she pointed out.

"So is that fan hanging from your wrist," he countered.

"I think," she said seriously, "that the country life is far more natural than this gay round of pleasure."

He held her from him and she saw that he too was adopting a serious mien.

"Are you trying to convince me that you are not enjoying your brilliant London Season, Miss Sherburn?"

"Oh, no, sir – not at all! On the contrary, I'm enjoying it immensely."

"Why then, are you finding fault with it?"

"I consider it should be a diversion rather than a regular way of life."

"I see." He appeared to be considering this, and no word was said between them for some time. Eleanor, thoroughly enjoying the dance, was content to remain quiet, busy as she was with her own thoughts. The Duchess, talking to her one afternoon when Beatrix was resting in her bedchamber, had told Eleanor a little about her nephew's vast estate in Kent. There were – in addition to the home farm itself – no less than two hundred other farms and smallholdings. Great areas of woodland extending almost to forest dimensions surrounded the pasture lands, and as for the mansion – this was so magnificent that she could not begin to describe it, her Grace had said.

"If only he would marry and settle down to looking after the estate," the Duchess had continued, "he would be a lot happier, I'm sure."

"Happier away from the gay round of London pleasure, ma'am?"

"I believe so. The trouble with Justin is that he is far too occupied with high-flyers! He's had his fling to my way of thinking , and it's time he gave up these wantons in favour of a nice little wife who'd be content to live in the country."

"But you yourself, ma'am? You appear to enjoy this life?"

"I've never been cut out for seclusion. Nevertheless, I advocate it for my nephew. There's something about him that troubles me. I often feel he's merely marking time, that he's basically bored with the whole frivolous goings on in London. Wait until you've been to Carlton House, and to the Brighton Pavilion. You'll deplore the ostentation. It's overbearing – positively oppressive!"

"You mean, the houses of the Prince?"

The Dowager had nodded vigorously.

"In Carlton House there isn't a spot that has not some finery embellishing it. Gold upon gold – all in the most deplorable taste! Every single apartment is vested with superfluous decoration." The Duchess had paused then, frowning heavily. "Ornate furniture, bronzes, gaudy porcelain, gold and silver plate. Can you tell me what can be more hideous than gold dragons everywhere, and gaudy Chinese lanterns, and nine-foot high pagodas? You'll see these latter when you pay your visit to the Pavilion."

Eleanor was left thinking of her Papa, who would assuredly deplore all this extravagance on the part of the Regent whose home, Carlton House, was said to be finer than anything else in the whole of the country, and not inferior in elegance and richness to Versailles or St Cloud.

Eleanor's musings were interrupted by the voice of her partner, saying again that she was very quiet.

"What are you thinking about?" he wanted to know, holding her a little way from him and looking down with a quizzical expression into her lovely face.

She hesitated, then, seeing no reason why she should not be frank – to a certain degree – she said quietly,

"You, my lord – at least, at first I was." His dark blue eyes were questioning and she added, "Your aunt, sir, was telling me about your estate in Kent."

"She was?" His lordship's eyes narrowed slightly. "Now why should she think that it would be of any interest to you?"

"I do not know, my lord. But she was in a confiding mood – the sort of mood you must have seen her in many times?" He merely nodded his head and she continued, "Her descriptions were rather attractive. I liked the idea of the vast expanse of pasturelands surrounded by forest. And she told me about your mansion; it must be very splendid indeed."

He made no response to this, and because, for some reason she was unable to fathom, she felt in a confiding mood herself, Eleanor went on to repeat his aunt's derisive descriptions of the Regent's homes. She noted with some surprise that several times during her narrative his lordship's head would nod in agreement.

"You yourself do not approve of all the splendour, my

lord?" she ventured to ask, but contrary to her expectations she received no answer. His lordship was now appearing bored, and she knew without any doubt at all that he was relieved when, the music having stopped, he could conduct her back to where his aunt was sitting.

CHAPTER
SIX

HER GRACE was surveying her nephew severely. Eleanor and Beatrix, seated on the sofa in the drawing-room, had glanced up on his entry a moment after the butler had announced him. Looking particularly splendid in his many-caped riding coat, and with his hair immaculately dressed in the style known as the Vanity Cut, his lordship's appearance brought a stifled gasp of admiration to Beatrix's lips.

"Isn't he grand?" she whispered.

"Hush!" warned Eleanor as the Dowager began to speak.

"You two children – run along. I desire to have a private talk with my nephew."

Rising instantly, the cousins glanced at one another, and then at the Marquis who, having strolled unconcernedly over to a table on which stood a decanter and several glasses, was now pouring out two drinks.

"May we take a walk?" asked Eleanor, her eyes following his lordship as he crossed the room to hand a glass of sherry to his aunt.

"Don't go far, and don't get yourselves tired. By rights you should both be resting, for we have a long evening ahead of us."

"The party at Carlton House," said Beatrix excitedly. "I do hope my lord Keddleston will be there!"

"Your flirtations are beginning to bore me, child," complained her Grace. "You came here to make a brilliant alliance, not to get yourself a bad name by flirting with every Sprig of Fashion in the city!"

Beatrix merely grinned, but behind her hand, and then turned to follow her cousin from the room.

"What do you suppose he's done to upset her?" Beatrix said, coming to a halt in the corridor a yard or two from the closed door of the drawing-room. "My, but she looks furiously angry."

Eleanor merely shrugged her shoulders.

"I couldn't even make a guess, Beatrix. Are you coming for a stroll?"

"No ..." Beatrix nevertheless fell into step beside her cousin. "I want to hear what's going on."

"You!" Eleanor stopped now, abruptly, and faced her cousin. "What did you say?" she demanded.

"I want to listen," replied Beatrix unashamedly.

A heavy frown settled upon Eleanor's forehead.

"You cannot be serious," she said severely. "No *nice* person listens to other people's conversation."

"Sometimes," returned Beatrix, "I am not at all a nice person."

"Come," urged Eleanor with a hint of impatience, "let us take that stroll."

"I'm going to listen," returned Beatrix obstinately. "If we go into the other drawing room, and slide back a small panel by the fireplace, we can hear everything that's being said between the Marquis and her Grace."

A gasp of incredulity was Eleanor's only response for a full thirty seconds.

"You mean – you have listened before?"

Beatrix said yes, she had.

"It's because I know that something odd is going on," she explained, quite unperturbed by the expression of utter disbelief that had settled on her cousin's face. "My aunt is up to something, Eleanor. Haven't you realized this before now – and with your acute brain, too? She's made you the rage –"

"Beatrix, please stop this nonsense," implored Eleanor. "There isn't anything strange going on –"

"You fibber! I'm sure that you know very well that there is! I'm going – I've wasted enough time, probably missing the most important part!" And before Eleanor could utter another word Beatrix was speeding along the corridor towards the door of the drawing-room next to the one from which they had just emerged.

"Oh, but this is scandalous of Beatrix!" she exclaimed softly to herself. "What ought I to do?"

Automatically she found herself moving towards the door through which her cousin had now disappeared. And she entered, driven by some force she could not combat. Beatrix was already in the act of sliding back the small panel she had mentioned, and she turned, putting one dainty finger to her lips.

"I can hear . . . hush . . ."

"I haven't yet said a word," began Eleanor hotly. "Come away, Beatrix!"

A frown was all she received from her cousin and with a shrug of helplessness she turned to the door.

"Eleanor – she's talking about you!" Beckoning, Beatrix tried to entice her cousin back again. But Eleanor shook her head. "Oh, come on –!"

"No, I wouldn't dream of listening!" Shocked and disgusted, Eleanor left the room. Half an hour later, having had her stroll, taking Eva with her, she returned to the house to find Beatrix waiting for her, her whole attitude one of excitement.

"I didn't discover everything," she told her cousin, "but I did hear plenty that will interest you!"

"I don't desire to hear it," returned Eleanor coldly. "Your conduct is disgraceful, Beatrix!"

"Fustian!" scoffed Beatrix. "We have every right to know what is going on!"

"I do not agree."

"It concerns you – and the Marquis."

Silence. Eleanor paled, and stared hard at her cousin.

"The Marquis . . . and me?" she repeated, quite unable to turn a deaf ear to what her cousin had to say.

"I will tell you it all – if you want to hear it, that is?"

Eleanor hesitated, guilt and curiosity and her sense of what was honourable all muddled up within her mind. She moistened her lips, seeing her Papa's stern set face – just as if he knew by some sort of telepathy of the conflict that was taking place within her.

"What was said about the Marquis and – and m-me?" she asked after a long and painful struggle.

Beatrix smiled, paused a second or two, and then related all that she had heard . . .

"I am of the opinion," her Grace had snapped, "that you are indulging in a flirtation with my protégée!"

"So . . .?"

"You don't attempt to deny it?"

"Why should I? Apparently you are not in any mood to listen to denials." The Marquis's voice was cool and faintly arrogant.

"I will not have it! Supposing the child should fall in love with you? So many women have – much to their cost!"

"I believe your provincial has far more sense than the rest."

"She has sense, I admit, but she hasn't seen anything; she knows nothing of the ways of men like you. Also, she's sure to be carried away by her unparalleled success, and will have come to the conclusion that a splendid marriage is not now out of the question."

The Marquis laughed.

"Are you implying that I'm the object of her ambitions?"

"It wouldn't be any use her setting her cap at you! In any case, haven't I often said that you'd make the most abominable husband imaginable?"

"You've also said that I ought to settle down, and live the life of a country squire."

"In my opinion that life would suit you admirably – but you won't even trouble to look around for a nice suitable wife."

"My love," protested his lordship, "you have just declared, most emphatically, that I should make the most abominable husband imaginable."

"Pah! You are trying to muddle me! You are also trying to fob me off! I won't have the subject changed, Justin. I want your solemn promise that you'll not flirt with the child."

"You'd deny me a little pleasant diversion?"

"Justin, I'm warning you! I shall cut you off!"

"Not again, my love," begged the Marquis imperturbably. "You know very well you think far too much about me to cut me off."

"Yes, in spite of your wicked ways there's something devilish attractive about you, Justin. I expect that's why the women fall so easily. A rake is always an attraction. However, to get back to my protégée. She's a helpless mite –"

"Helpless? My dear Aunt Lucy, I must correct you there. Miss Sherburn can take good care of herself, I assure you."

"You haven't assured me! You know, Justin, one of these days you're going to meet your match – and change your dissolute ways!"

"Not a chance!" The Marquis paused a moment. "Am I to take it that you no longer want it to appear that she basks in my favour?"

"You tiresome creature – no! That is not what I mean at

all. She will continue to bask in your favour at balls and routs and the rest, but you needn't take her out *quite* so much."

"She's going to consider it rather odd if I begin to neglect her."

"You won't be neglecting her. As I've said, you'll attend her at functions as usual. And you will still drive her out, but not every day as you have been doing."

Beatrix came to a stop at this point, an expression of vexation on her pretty face.

"I didn't hear any more. They had another drink and when they resumed talking they'd moved out on to the verandah. Eleanor, what does it all mean?"

As Eleanor turned the conversation over in her mind, one part seemed to leap out at her and she whispered to herself,

"Supposing the child should fall in love with you ..."

Fall in love ... with the handsome Marquis of Trouvaine ... Eleanor faced the fact that she had, on more than one occasion, experienced strange stirrings within her – the sudden rush of blood in her veins, or a quickening of the senses. More recently – only the previous day in fact, when she had been driving in the Park with his lordship, and the horses had jerked on being confronted by a huge aggressive hound, she had known a thrill of excitement as, being thrown against her companion, she had felt his supporting arm come instantly around her. Her heart had raced, and she had turned from him, she recalled, being afraid to let him read her expression. "No," she whispered, "I have more sense than to fall in love with one so exalted as his lordship. Why, he said so himself: he said I had far more sense than the rest."

"Eleanor – I've asked you what it means!" The insistent voice of her cousin brought Eleanor from her reverie and she glanced up, frowning.

"It would appear that the Duchess is afraid that her nephew will flirt with me –"

"Not that part of it," interrupted Beatrix impatiently. "That's plain enough! What did his lordship mean when he suggested that my aunt no longer wanted it to appear that you are basking in his favour?"

Eleanor shook her head, having no notion how she could answer a question like this. Then it dawned on her quite suddenly that, had she herself not overheard a conversation between the Duchess and her nephew, she would have been just as bewildered as her cousin. And in consequence she said, shrugging her shoulders in a gesture of puzzlement,

"It is difficult to guess what he meant."

"It doesn't seem possible that my aunt would request him to dance attendance upon you, yet it is perfectly plain that she has done so."

"Yes, it is," was all Eleanor could find to say.

"I shall find out what it all means," declared Beatrix with far more determination and forcefulness than Eleanor had ever encountered in her before. Beatrix was normally of a placid nature, never taking much interest in things which did not affect her personally. "It will be fun, solving a mystery, don't you think?"

"We ought not to probe into her Grace's business," began Eleanor, when her cousin interrupted her.

"It appears to be your business also, Eleanor. I am of the opinion that you are being used – in fact, it's very obvious that you are. However, for the present we shall have to contain our curiosity." Beatrix paused a moment, looking at her cousin, examining her face and her hair and her lovely figure – a figure enchantingly clad in a gown of sprigged muslin with crepe trimmings and flowers round the bottom of the skirt. "Do you suppose the Marquis finds you attractive, Eleanor?" she murmured at last, and Eleanor gave a swift, spasmodic start.

"No, of course not! What gave you an idea like that, I wonder!"

"He wouldn't want to flirt with you otherwise."

Eleanor shook her head. She desired only to bring this conversation to a speedy end.

"The Marquis wouldn't look at me in *that* way," she said.

"Well, at least we know why he's been dancing attendance on you all this while – it was at the request of my aunt who, for some reason of her own, was determined to make you the rage. She succeeded, no doubt about that. But *why* did she want to make you the rage? I have a good mind to ask her outright!"

"Beatrix, you have just said that, for the present, you'll have to contain your curiosity. Your aunt would only give you a set-down were you to approach her with a question like that. And have you thought that she might then guess that you've eavesdropped on her conversation with his lordship?"

Beatrix frowned, biting her lip.

"You are right, Eleanor. Oh, but it is a strange mystery!"

Remaining silent, Eleanor hoped that this exclamation would be the end of the matter, but she was mistaken. Beatrix began to warn her about the Marquis, advising her to keep him at a distance.

"It would be just too dreadful if, as my dear aunt fears, you fell in love with him," Beatrix went on. "It isn't as if you could ever hope to win him for your husband – not with your expectations being what they are. So do, I beg of you, *dearest* Eleanor, be on your guard. I should hate it above all things if you were to be hurt, which you must be, were it to transpire that you had a *tendre* for him."

"You have no need to worry," returned Eleanor rather stiffly. "I know what I'm about where his lordship is concerned. I would have you know that, whenever we are out driving in his curricle, we invariably quarrel."

"You ...?" Beatrix stared disbelievingly at her. "But, dearest cousin, *you* never quarrel with anyone!"

"I never *did* quarrel with anyone. I certainly do now."

"It isn't possible. You would not dream of saying anything that would lead to a quarrel."

"With his lordship I would."

"You're funning me!"

"No such thing. The Marquis and I seem to irritate one another."

"Then why does he call for you and take you driving? It isn't as if he's forced to pander to her Grace's wishes."

"Perhaps he likes our little sparring matches."

Beatrix's big blue eyes took on a sceptical look.

"You *are* funning me," she accused. "For one thing, his lordship is far too forbidding for you to risk displeasing him."

"I'm afraid," returned her cousin, "that he is easily displeased."

"You mean – he takes exception to all that you say to him?"

"Not all, but we do usually end up by sitting in silence – and it's without doubt a *sulky* silence on his part."

"I don't believe it! His lordship has the most amiable temperament!"

"It isn't long since you were branding him odious," her cousin reminded her in tones of accusation. "And now you're praising him. You have very soon forgotten the horrid things he said about me – referring to me as the provincial, which he did again just an hour or so ago. He never refers to you in that most derogatory manner."

"Well, you know, Eleanor, *he* is aware of my superior situation. After all, I am my dear Papa's only child."

"What does that signify? You're still a provincial."

"I don't expect he really means to be insulting," decided her cousin after some thought. "He is a *gentleman*, remember."

Her cousin looked strangely at her.

"You've certainly changed your opinion of him, Beatrix," she said severely.

"Oh, I have not a *tendre* for him, if that is what you are insinuating," she protested indignantly, yet for all that there lurked in her eyes a tell-tale expression which set her denial at nought. "His Grace of Mordelay is my latest beau; you are fully aware of that fact, Eleanor." Her cousin made no comment on this. She was becoming convinced that, deep down inside her, Beatrix was finding the Marquis inordinately attractive. "Mama declared I should have many London beaux, and you must admit that I have!"

"Indeed, yes."

"So have you, of course." Another pause and then, "Do you know, Eleanor, it is quite the oddest thing, but I do not feel any anger that my aunt has made you all the rage."

"I'm relieved," returned her cousin a little drily. She was – much to her surprise – losing patience with Beatrix, just as her Mama had so often lost patience with her.

"You see," continued her cousin with a smile, "I am not of the disposition to be *envious* of anyone!"

"Again I'm relieved."

"Now you're being horrid with me!"

Eleanor sighed, and after a while she excused herself, saying she must have a rest in preparation for the evening's big event, which was the dinner party at Carlton House to which the Duchess and her two protégées had been invited.

When she was dressed in readiness for the party, Eleanor looked at herself in the full-length mirror fixed to the wall of her bedchamber.

"Miss," Eva had exclaimed several times during the past hour and a quarter, "you will be the *star* tonight!"

The gown, of ruched satin of a shade between coral and peach, was trimmed with tiny pearls which formed curves beneath her small, high breasts, meeting at the front in a rosette from which hung several lengths of soft green ribbon. Her jewellery consisted of a diamond necklace with matching eardrops and bracelet, all lent by the Dowager.

"It is very beautiful," breathed Eleanor softly as she lifted a fold of the gown and fingered the material.

"It's the most *ravishingly* beautiful gown!" declared the smiling maid. "The colour was made just for *your* particular colouring, Miss. It's no wonder brunettes have come into fashion. It could not be otherwise with you making your debut. Your influence has been incredible! All the young ladies with blonde hair must be grinding their teeth at their loss of popularity."

Frowning at this, because she knew her Papa would be filled with contempt on hearing such words, Eleanor said nothing, merely reaching out to accept from Eva's hand the dainty matching reticule of satin and pearls, and the antique fan which the Duchess herself had used when she was a young debutante.

One of the first persons she encountered on entering the Circular Room of the Regent's London residence was Lady Tiernay who, sweeping down upon the Dowager and her party, which included the Marquis and Lord Furnese – another of Beatrix's beaux and a close friend of the Marquis – greeted Eleanor with the words,

"I felt, on seeing you enter, that I must come over and congratulate you on your perfectly enchanting gown!"

Somewhat taken aback by this unexpected show of affability, Eleanor found difficulty in framing a suitable response, and quite unconsciously lifted her head to look into his lordship's face, as if beseeching him to answer for her.

"My aunt's protégée is rendered speechless by your kind words of appreciation, ma'am," said the Marquis suavely and without a second's hesitation. "I myself must agree that she is looking delightful tonight ... but then, she always does." And his dark blue eyes held the strangest expression as they looked with a piercing regard into those of the beautiful girl at his side.

"Now what was her little game?" the Dowager was demanding of her nephew a short while later when, Lord Furnese having gallantly taken Beatrix off to explore the many ornate corridors and apartments, the Duchess and Eleanor and his lordship were in one of the withdrawing-rooms waiting for the approach of the Prince who, being the excellent host that he was, rarely failed to have a few words with all his guests.

"It was merely for effect," replied the Marquis. "So many notables were about, and as it is common knowledge that Miss Sherburn has ousted the Incomparable it might be surmised that her ladyship is harbouring a grudge against you."

The Dowager laughed.

"And does she conclude that the approach she made will give the lie to that?"

Eleanor, naturally experiencing a large measure of embarrassment by this outspokenness, again looked up into Lord Trouvaine's face, silently pleading with him to change the subject. As before his eyes flickered with that strange unfathomable light, and as before he obliged her by granting her unspoken wish.

"It's of no consequence, my love," he said to his aunt. "Ah, here comes Prinny himself. Miss Sherburn, you are shortly to experience your finest moment." But, as she allowed her eyes to wander to the obese figure approaching them, she was asking herself if she had only imagined it, or if there really was a hint of contempt in his lordship's voice. The Prince was all smiles; he chatted for a few moments before moving on, to extend a welcome to the Duke of Sandwick and his exquisitely beautiful French wife.

"Well?" inquired the Marquis with a sardonic curve of his lips. "Were you duly impressed by the man who one day will be our king?"

She set her mouth, longing to express her real opinion of the man whose entire life was spent in the pursuit of pleasure. However, she had now been in London long enough to know that etiquette and total decorum must be maintained no matter what one's private thoughts were, so she merely produced a casual smile and said,

"It was gracious of him to comment on my appearance."

The Marquis laughed; she looked at the lines running from nose to chin, and those fanning out at the corners of his eyes, and once again she observed that he was the most attractively handsome gentleman who had ever come her way. But at the same time she was acutely conscious of the disparaging things he had said about her; she knew also that he was indulging in a flirtation, since he had actually admitted it when he inquired of the Duchess if she would deny him a little pleasant diversion. These words, which she would never have known about had not Beatrix insisted on eavesdropping, had persistently come into the forefront of Eleanor's mind; she had pondered them for long periods, and had at last decided that all she could do was continue to adopt the cool and indifferent attitude towards him. He would tire soon; he would accept defeat before she did; he would retire in a fit of umbrage. But not yet, for he was obviously still intending to pander to his aunt's whim; otherwise he would not have accompanied them here tonight, but would instead have attended the dinner in the company of one or other of his friends.

"Very diplomatically put," the Marquis was saying in response to her guarded words about the Prince. "If I might say it, Miss Sherburn, it would be more becoming in you were you equally guarded when expressing your opinion of me."

A silence fell, the silence of disbelief. It was broken at length by the Duchess, who inquired of her nephew just what he meant by that remark.

"I have heard you giving some of your severest set-downs to those who vex or anger you, but never have I known you to exhibit rudeness where no provocation has occurred. I hate to think what poor Eleanor's secret reaction must be!"

Eleanor, catching the amusement in his lordship's eye, was not one whit surprised by his answer.

"Have no fears about the child's sensibilities, ma'am. She and I understand each other. For us to have a dig at one another is the rule rather than the exception."

"Is this true?" frowned the Dowager, looking to her protégée for confirmation. Eleanor – although she would dearly have loved to make a denial, just for the pleasure of hearing the Marquis receive the sharp end of his aunt's tongue – nodded her head and said yes, this certainly was true. "Then by all means allow me to congratulate you," her Grace added. "You must be the first woman who has had the courage to indulge in a battle of words with my nephew!" The old lady looked at her with an expression both curious and admiring. "The fact that this sparring in words appears to be a regular occurrence is proof that my nephew must have practised the greatest restraint, since otherwise you'd have retired long before now."

"Admitting defeat, ma'am?" The words were out before Eleanor could prevent them, spoken with indignation and accompanied by a vigorous shake of the head. "Never!"

Another silence ensued before the Dowager said, looking first at Eleanor, then at her nephew,

"Well, well ... To have a female – and one scarcely out of the schoolroom – stand up for herself must be a most chastening experience for you, my lord?"

The Marquis, who had been surveying the flamboyant furnishings of the room through his quizzing glass while at the same time giving much of his attention to what his august relative was saying, replied without a second's hesitation,

"Indeed it is, your Grace, and a novel one to boot."

In spite of herself Eleanor had to laugh.

"You are being nonsensical, my lord!" she admonished.

He turned then, and gave her his full attention, while the Duchess, definitely intrigued by all this, ignored the flunkey who, with a silver tray in his hand, was silently inviting her to partake of a glass of Madeira wine, and watched with narrowed eyes the glances exchanged between her enchanting protégée and the tall distinguished nobleman who for more than ten years past had remained one of Society's most eligible bachelors, the target for mumerous hopeful Mamas whose aim it was to break through the barrier of indifference he invariably adopted towards their lovely young daughters.

"And you," his lordship retorted at last, "are, as is customary, being impertinent. Were I your brother, ma'am, I should have cured you a long time ago!"

At which the colour rushed to his adversary's delicate cheeks, and incredulity to the Dowager's pale blue eyes.

"My lord," this lady exclaimed in stiff admonishing tones, "it is more than plain to me that you ask for what you receive!"

"Undoubtedly, my love," he returned cheerfully. "One dig gives rise to another, and so it goes on." He laughed as he looked down into Eleanor's flushed face. "Is that not so, Miss Sherburn?"

She sent him a furious glance before replying, her voice quivering with indignation,

"You invariably provoke me, sir! And without exception it is you who start the argument!"

"My children," interposed the Dowager hastily, "pray cease your wrangling, for here comes his Grace the Duke of Clarence!" The Marquis turned his head, while Eleanor, flicking open her fan, began with some urgency to cool her burning cheeks. The royal Duke was in truth making for the place where the three were standing.

Bowing low over the Duchess's hand, he then turned, so that Eleanor could be presented to him. As was the case with his brother the Regent, the Duke stayed for a few moments before moving away, making for a group of Corinthians of whom Beau Brummell was the central figure.

"What a coarse and uncouth man!" Eleanor spoke softly, but without prior thought, as the Duchess raised a warning finger to her lips.

"It is more than clear that our royal family is not finding favour with you," commented his lordship, raising his quizzing glass and appearing to be making a critical examination of the Duke's satin coat with its medley of gold trimmings. A dark frown crossed the Marquis's forehead and from his half-closed lips there escaped a single word which Eleanor was almost certain was "Deplorable!"

"I do think, my lord," responded Eleanor when the Marquis returned his attention to her, "that royalty should lead us all in matters of courtesy, manners and good taste!"

His lordship's eyes opened wide, as did his aunt's.

"Is that all your own, ma'am – or Papa's?"

Having cooled her cheeks, Eleanor found them becoming warm again.

"In all honesty the words were originally Papa's," she

owned, but added that they were not used in connection
with royalty.

"In the pulpit, I expect," suggested her Grace and
Eleanor said yes, this was so.

Nothing more was said, as at that moment Beatrix and her
escort appeared, having made an exploratory visit to several
of the rooms.

"The place is quite fantastic!" exclaimed Beatrix. "The
Prince must be one of the wealthiest men in the world to
be able to afford all this!" Sweeping a hand she indicated
the ornate ceiling, the white walls lavishly decorated with
gold leaf, the heavily gilded pelmets, the Dolphin furniture
with its rich gilt embellishments.

Eleanor and the Marquis exchanged glances; she wondered if he were thinking what she herself was thinking —
that the Prince Regent was about two million pounds in
debt.

The table in the banqueting-room was enough to make
any young girl of Eleanor's upbringing gasp with amazement.
Beatrix too gave an audible exclamation on entering the
most incredibly spectacular of all the royal apartments
in Carlton House. The long table glittered with gold and
silver plate, with engraved candelabra, with glass and
porcelain, with exquisitely-embroidered linen, with flowers
of every hue. As for the room, this also was breathtaking
in its ornateness. Three-dimensional effects of trees and
flowers and animals, all ostentatiously decorated with gold
leaf and pearls and other jewels, were everywhere boldly
displayed. It was just too overpowering, Eleanor thought,
actually giving a small shudder which the Marquis noticed.

The menu, consisting of no less than ninety-two dishes,
was, to Eleanor's mind absolutely absurd. It was no wonder
these people suffered from gout and all sorts of other
ailments – eating in this gluttonous manner.

"I pray you, Miss Sherburn," commented the Marquis

who was sitting on her right, "do not reveal your disapproval as plainly as you are doing.'"

"It is all too ridiculous, my lord," she said. "What does anyone want with ninety-two dishes from which to choose? Why, one ought to be sent the menu in advance – a week in advance!"

"I agree," he said, surprising her. "It might interest you to know that, at one banquet held at the Brighton Pavilion, there were over a hundred and twenty dishes."

She stared at him incredulously.

"It is madness, sir!"

Again he agreed. And for the duration of the meal he and she conversed in a more friendly way than ever before.

CHAPTER
SEVEN

THE Dowager, sitting opposite them at the dinner table, several times cast her eyes in their direction. Catching these glances, Eleanor believed she knew the reason for them: her Grace was keeping a watchful eye on her nephew, just to make sure he did not flirt with her. That he himself also believed this to be the reason for these glances was evident in the quizzical manner in which he returned them.

A long time afterwards Eleanor again found herself close to the Marquis. He had been conversing with his friend, Mr Brummell, who was now dallying with Lady Jersey, but on seeing Eleanor making for the open air his lordship instantly followed. He caught up with her when, on reaching a fountain, she stopped to take in several breaths of the cool clear air.

"You are unwell?" He sounded anxious, she thought, her big brown eyes faintly questioning as she raised them to his.

"No, not in the least, my lord, but it is far too hot and stuffy inside. How do they endure it?"

A faint, contemptuous smile curved the Marquis's lips.

"Prinny would hardly be flattered to hear the word 'endure', Miss Sherburn."

"For me it was an endurance! All those thousands of candles! – and the fires also! It was too much, my lord!"

She was fanning herself with pretty movements of the wrist; his lordship stood above her, very close. Tall and straight and distinguished-looking, he was a perfect example of nobility and good taste, his attire being immaculate and yet, like that of the Beau, depending on excellent cut rather than decoration or anything out of the ordinary.

"Allow me to get you something to drink, ma'am," he said with a smile. "You will feel much refreshed by a glass of lemonade, I'm sure."

"Thank you, sir," she returned gratefully, still employing her fan even though a cooling breeze was blowing up from the west. She watched the Marquis as he strolled unhurriedly towards the area where supper tables had been laid out beside a miniature cascade and lily pond. On his return he had two glasses, one containing lemonade, the other filled with champagne.

"Shall we sit over there, beneath those trees?" he suggested and she nodded her assent. Once seated, he stretched out his long legs in front of him, teetering back on his chair and staring thoughtfully into his glass, appearing to be watching the bubbles as they rose to the surface.

"So you haven't really enjoyed your first visit to Carlton House?" he enquired after what seemed an eternity.

"It was an experience, my lord, which I wouldn't have missed," she was honest enough to confess. "It will make interesting reading for Mama when next I write to her. She will be most surprised that the Prince and his brother both spoke to me."

"The Duke of Clarence appeared to be rather more than interested in you," he commented in a dry and faintly sardonic tone.

She frowned at this.

"I did not notice, my lord," she said.

"His eyes have followed you on many occasions this evening," the Marquis informed her. "Any other young female would have been in transports – yet you never even notice. Of a surety, Miss Sherburn, you are *different*."

She glanced up quickly.

"Different from what, my lord?"

His eyes narrowed; she coloured daintily.

"Be a little more explicit, ma'am!" he almost snapped.

She paused, but not for long. As he had mentioned to his aunt, she and he understood one another.

"Your lights o'love, my lord? Were you meaning that I was different from them?"

She thought for one fearful moment that he would lose all sense of correctness and smack her, hard.

"How dare you mention those women to me! Madam, you will have to restrain that tongue of yours if you wish to keep your place at the top!"

She sipped her lemonade in silence, aware that, this time, she was not happy with the way he was treating her. Until now they had actually derived some measure of enjoyment from their battles of words; but suddenly she was finding that she wanted nothing more than that they should converse on more amiable terms.

"I'm sorry, my lord," she said meekly at length. "I'm afraid I sometimes go too far."

"You often go too far!" he was swift to correct her. "You do realize, Miss Sherburn, that were I to withdraw my interest in you, you would no longer keep your popularity?"

She nodded her head, lowering her beautiful dark eyelashes, so as to conceal her embarrassment from him. She said in a subdued voice, thinking of the Duchess and the triumph she was at present enjoying,

"I hope, sir, that you will not withdraw it?"

For a long time he looked at her profile, taking in the lovely classical lines, portraying character at its most attractive. Mentally he compared her beauty with that of her cousin. Airy-fairy prettiness, he thought.

A sigh escaped him, causing Eleanor to turn her head sharply; she was curious to learn what had prompted the sigh. Their eyes met, and held for a long moment. Something within her seemed to set a spark alight; she felt her pulse increase, her heart begin to beat over-rate. The silence became intense, filled with a strange power that seemed to affect them both, to hold them motionless, unsmiling, yet so close as to be almost intimate. She had to break that unbearable silence, yet words were difficult, for her throat felt stiff, her tongue dry.

"You haven't answered me, sir," she managed to utter at last and she saw by the sudden puckering of his forehead that he was having to concentrate to recall what it was she had said to him.

"Yes – do not fear, Miss Sherburn, I shall continue to pay court to you."

"Thank you, my lord."

His eyes still held hers; after another thoughtful interlude he said, the most odd inflection in his finely-modulated voice,

"It has just struck me, Miss Sherburn, that not once have you evinced the least measure of surprise that I should afford you so much of my time."

Strangely, she herself had been rather puzzled that this question had not occurred before now – seeing that she and the Marquis were so outspoken with one another.

"I have an idea," she said, feeling that, as his lordship had long since credited her with above average intelligence, it was useless to assume a naïve and bewildered manner now, "that the Duchess desired that I become the rage."

His lordship took a drink of his champagne.

"I suppose that was bound to strike you," he said.

Eleanor nodded.

"She mentioned that I would be, you see. Also, she has gone out of her way to fit me out in clothes which are the very height of fashion."

"You were fitted out by your parents, though?" he said, for the moment diverted.

"Oh, yes, but I did come as a companion to my cousin,

you know. True, I was to be brought out, for her Grace generously offered to do this great kindness for me, but it was for Beatrix's sake that we came here, as you already know, my lord."

He nodded absently.

"It will be a miracle if your cousin makes that brilliant match her Mama has in mind. She is already gaining the nickname *Coquette* –"

"No! Oh, this is not so, surely! You're quizzing me, sir!" But he was already shaking his head.

"She soon forgot her Hugh," he commented drily. "She is so like all the rest."

Eleanor looked at him, recalling what his aunt had said about his cynicism.

"I feel that you are disillusioned, sir," she remarked before she could stop herself. "All women are not alike; it's inconceivable that you should have reached a conclusion of that kind."

"How do you know what conclusion I have reached?"

She shrugged her shoulders, taking another couple of sips of her lemonade before answering.

"I can tell by your manner, and by remarks you make at various times."

He smiled then, and his face cleared. He was no longer thoughtful or pensively withdrawn from her.

"This is what comes of being a man of the world, Miss Sherburn. Tell me about your family," he added, changing the subject with an abruptness that startled her for the moment.

"You would not be interested, my lord. We are not in any way anything out of the ordinary."

"Tell me, nevertheless," he said imperiously.

Puzzled, but surprised by his sudden demand for obedience, she began to tell him about her Papa. Then she talked of her Mama, mentioning quite casually that she came from a family much higher in the social scale than her husband.

"It was a love match, though," added Eleanor with a sudden happy smile. "They are poor, but so very happy together. You have no idea, sir, what it is like to live in a home where there is so much love!"

"Very true, I have not," returned his lordship gravely.

"Oh dear," she cried in tones of swift distress, "my tongue again, sir! What made me phrase it in that particular way?"

The Marquis's fine lips twitched.

"Because, Miss Sherburn, you never stop to think!"

"You are so right, my lord," she quivered. "Mama used to say that my tongue would get me into serious trouble one day."

"I shouldn't allow it to worry you overmuch," he advised soothingly. "Tell me some more about your family."

"I have a brother; he is hoping to go up to Oxford."

The Marquis nodded.

"You have other brothers and sisters?"

"One sister, Augusta. She is married to a gentleman who owns a small estate in Derbyshire. They are very happy also, another love match, you understand?"

"So your parents did not aspire for great things for your sister? They allowed her to marry the man of her own choice?"

"That's right, my lord."

"And you, Miss Sherburn," he said, and now his voice had taken on a softer, almost gentle tone. "Shall they allow you to marry for love?"

"I sincerely hope so," she answered, vaguely wondering why a picture of life with the Marquis should rise instantly before her. "As I have always remarked to my cousin, I cannot conceive what it would be like, being married to someone you did not love."

A small and unfathomable silence followed before his
lordship said, in so quiet a tone that she had to strain her
ears to catch his words,

"Nor can I . . . no, nor can I . . ."

Many times during the following days these unexpected
words came back to Eleanor; she knew by their very
utterance that there was far more to his lordship than lay
on the surface, that he possessed hidden depths which
very few people had discovered. On the surface he was an
idler, an Arbiter of Fashion, an eligible Corinthian, a Leader
of Society. Favoured by nature with a handsome face and perfect physique, the owner of a vast estate and fortune, it was no
wonder that such a Nonpareil should be doted on by his
contemporaries. Basking as he did in the favour of royalty,
it had been a simple matter for him to drift into the
frivolous ways of those with whom he continually came into
contact. A member of the Four-in-Hand Club, the Carlton
House Set, the Bow-window Set and all the rest, he had
little time to spend on the serious things of life.

The more she dwelt on all this the more Eleanor found
herself agreeing with the Duchess that his lordship ought
to look round for a wife and settle down to run his country
estate. She thought of Beatrix, deciding almost at once that
she would not do at all for my lord; he would desire a lady
far more serious in her ways, more sensible and mature.

Again the picture of life with him rose before her; she
knew again that increase of the pulse, but in addition her
mind was in a whirl, as if all rational thought had been
swamped by a dream . . . the dream of –

"No! I must not think of such absurd impossibilities!
What is the matter with me that I can even harbour such
improbable ideas?" Her mind still in a state of agitation,
she turned as a knock on the door of her bedchamber
reminded her that it was time to dress for her drive in the

Park with his lordship. "I d-do not want to go," she faltered, shaking her head as if by so doing she could send Eva away – with a message for the Marquis expressing her regret that she could not go out driving with him today ... or at any other time, for that matter. The knock came again; she called quietly,

"Come in," and turned away swiftly to conceal her expression even from the maid.

"A pretty bouquet of flowers for you, Miss," pronounced Eva in her customary exuberant fashion. "From his lordship the Earl of Brockheath!" Displaying the card before the startled eyes of her mistress, Eva went on to say that this was success indeed. "Just supposing he offers for you, Miss! What a triumph! He's one of the richest gentlemen in the whole of England!"

Taking the card in fingers that trembled, Eleanor stared disbelievingly at it. True, Isobel's beau had began to display some interest in Eleanor some while ago, but never had he given her an indication that he had a *tendre* for her. Yet she had heard it said of him that he had once declared – quite emphatically – that he would send flowers only to the girl with whom he fell in love.

The bouquet itself was lovely, and after handling it with a sort of tenderness she had learned from her Mama, she gave it to the maid, requesting her to arrange the flowers daintily in water and put them on her dressing-table.

For riding, Eleanor put on a fine cambric dress over which she wore a mantle of soft velvet with a hood lined with taffeta. Her curls were dressed in a style that kept them up high, secured by a wide silk riband. Gloves that bore the stamp of France, and a reticule to match, were handed to her by Eva, and with one final glance in the mirror she left the room and went down to the drawing-room to await his lordship's appearance.

The Dowager was there, looking very regal in a gown of

figured French silk and with a Norwich shawl about her shoulders. Looking up as Eleanor entered the room, she allowed her eyes to wander critically over her slender figure.

"Very charming," she announced after a while. "You liked the posy sent to you by the Earl?"

"Very much, ma'am." Eleanor, fidgeting with the gloves she had not yet drawn on to her hands, hesitated a moment, trying to frame her words. "Ma'am," she began at last, "it is not the thing for the Earl to send me flowers."

The Duchess blinked.

"Why not, my child?"

"Because I cannot ever mean anything to him, ma'am. He – he once said that he would never send flowers to any female other than the one he fell in love with."

This was not news to her Grace; Eleanor saw it at once, by her expression.

"And why, my child, cannot you mean anything to him?"

Spreading her hands at this mildly spoken question, Eleanor stared at her Grace in some considerable surprise.

"Ma'am, you know it is not possible for me to make a brilliant match."

The Dowager, receiving this without so much as the bat of an eyelid, said composedly,

"If you are thinking of your situation, then forget it, Eleanor. "It isn't unknown for a young female of particularly outstanding beauty to land for herself a nobleman of high rank. I see no reason to suppose that the Earl is trifling with you – in fact, he has already approached me with hints that he would like to address you –"

"Oh, no!" Distressed and with her mouth quivering, Eleanor made a stronger protest than before, pointing out that she had never been brought up to be one of the ton, that even if this miracle should occur she would not know how to behave among the people of the Nobility.

"Fustian!" was all she received from her Grace. "You have the prettiest manners, have entered the Polite World without any difficulties whatsoever. I am of the opinion that you should encourage the Earl, whose intentions are of the most honourable."

Eleanor shook her head, wishing she could inform the Duchess that she knew of her scheme, was fully aware that any offer she received from the nobleman who Lady Tiernay had expected would offer for her granddaughter, would be the crowning point of the Duchess's success. However, as this was not possible, Eleanor resorted to a firm but polite disagreement with her Grace's opinion.

"Do you not owe it to your parents to take advantage of your rise to popularity?" said the Dowager quietly when at length Eleanor had come to an end of her pro-testations.

"Mama has never expected me to marry into the ton, ma'am," returned Eleanor gravely. "I would not deny that it would delight her if I did so, but she has always been resigned to my marrying someone like Algernon – that is my sister's husband," she elucidated. "He has a comfor-table income . . ." Her voice trailed away and she turned her head. The Duchess also turned. The Marquis was standing just inside the door, having entered unseen and unheard by both occupants of the room.

"Justin," protested her Grace shortly, "what do you mean by creeping about in my house?"

"Beg pardon, Aunt Lucy, but as there was an absence of both butler and footmen I came right in." His voice was oddly taut. His dark blue eyes had settled on Eleanor's face; framed as it was by the hood, with her pretty hair spilling from around it, she presented a picture so enchant-ing that he had the greatest difficulty in withdrawing his gaze from her when, again addressed by his aunt, he was forced to pay her some attention.

"Pray tell me, how much have you heard of our conversation, my lord?"

"Enough to have learned that the Earl of Brockheath's offer for Miss Sherburn's hand is imminent." Again that taut edge to his voice, and his eyes had narrowed almost to slits. With a sort of regal swing to his gait he advanced further into the elegant drawing-room and stood by an elbow chair of richly carved oak, but he made no attempt to take possession of it. Dressed in a riding coat of many capes, he made the most impressive figure, and Eleanor turned away, conscious of sensations both disturbing and profound. Was she being so unwise as to fall in love with his lordship? She tried to dismiss the thought but it persisted; she found herself torn between resignation and denial. She was not so foolish as to fall in love with him! she told herself vehemently. And yet she wished she had never met him . . .

"The Earl has sent flowers to Eleanor," the Duchess informed him. "I think that perhaps you have heard his famous remark that he would never send flowers to any lady other than the one he wished to marry?"

"I've heard something of the sort," replied the Marquis impatiently. "Miss Sherburn, I am ready when you are."

She nodded, and managed a smile, but before she could speak the Dowager was saying, an odd inflection in her voice,

"You don't appear to be all joy that Eleanor has gained the interest of one of the Season's most eligible bachelors."

"All joy?" he repeated with an arrogant lift of his brows. "Why the devil should I care – one way or the other?"

"Justin! Remember where you are! What language to use in the presence of ladies –!"

"Fustian! You yourself have often used worse."

The Dowager's pale blue eyes glinted.

"Eleanor is a Vicar's daughter, sir! Kindly keep that in mind!"

He glanced at Eleanor.

"I beg your pardon, ma'am," he said stiffly.

She remained silent, feeling that this was the more prudent thing to do. However, that she was suffering acute embarrassment went without saying; she did wish the Duchess would not keep on presuming that she could marry so advantageously.

"Apart from the bad language you have used," went on the Duchess, "you were also most uncivil to Eleanor. For even if as you say you do not care one way or the other, you had no need to voice it – at least, not in her presence."

"Ma'am," interposed Eleanor in beseeching tones, "please let the subject drop."

To her relief her Grace nodded, realizing at last that all this was causing her protégée some discomfiture.

"Off you go, then, and have an enjoyable drive."

As it happened the drive was far from pleasant. His lordship was so long silent that Eleanor began to wonder if he intended speaking to her at all. Several times she turned her head, but he kept his eyes either on the road or on his horses. James, the undersized but wiry boy groom known as a "tiger", merely grimaced when, on turning her head right round, Eleanor looked at him, sitting there, upright at the back. In the Park, his lordship was continually nodding his head, or lifting a hand, in acknowledgment of greetings from friends and acquaintances. The Duke of Clarence was driving with Mrs Jordan, gifted actress and mother of his many illegitimate children; Beau Brummell was another who passed greetings to his lordship; that Dandy, the Earl of Leily, attired so gaudily that Eleanor could not help exclaiming, also hailed the Marquis, inquiring if he would be at Watier's the following evening. The Marquis frowningly shook his head and drove on.

At last Eleanor could bear it no longer and, risking one of his lordship's caustic rejoinders, she asked him if anything were troubling him.

"Why should it be?" he retorted curtly, without turning his head.

"You're so quiet, my lord."

"I am often quiet."

She sighed, and presently said, her dignity coming to the fore,

"Would you mind, sir, if we did not continue our drive? I think I would like to be taken back to Cavendish Square."

He did turn then, abruptly.

"You are not enjoying the drive?"

"I prefer to go home, my lord."

"As you wish, ma'am," he said and, reining in to allow a fashionable barouche to pass him, he turned his horses.

Beatrix was with the Duchess when Eleanor arrived back at Cavendish Square; both glanced up in surprise, their eyes looking beyond her shoulders for the tall figure of the Marquis.

"Where is my nephew?" enquired the Duchess after listening to Eleanor explaining that she had desired to be brought home.

"He's gone, ma'am," replied Eleanor flinging back her hood and shaking out her curls. She was feeling so dejected she could have taken herself off and indulged in a fit of the vapours, but as this was against her ideas of commonsense she put on a brave face, smiling almost cheerfully at her Grace. "I expect he felt there was no need for him to accompany me any further than the front door. He asked me to convey the message that he would not be at the theatre on Wednesday after all."

A small silence followed, with both her Grace and

Beatrix looking oddly at Eleanor as she stood there, in the middle of the luxurious room, unfastening her cloak.

"But he promised to escort us to Drury Lane," said the Duchess at last. "It's the strangest thing that he should change his mind. Whatever my nephew's faults he invariably keeps his promises." Her regard was piercing but Eleanor met it unflinchingly. "Have you and the Marquis quarrelled?" her Grace asked bluntly, and this did put her protégée out of countenance; she blushed, so that all was given away. And yet, on pondering the matter for a moment, Eleanor found that she could not with truth say that a quarrel had taken place between the Marquis and herself.

"Well . . . it was not a quarrel exactly, ma'am."

"But you did have a disagreement?" Her Grace was decidedly interested and her expression more than revealed this fact.

"If you please, ma'am," said Eleanor agitatedly, "I would rather not speak about it."

The Dowager frowned, but it was Beatrix who spoke, taking no notice at all of her cousin's words.

"It sounds as if you have displeased his lordship, dear Eleanor. What a shame! His interest in you was what really took you to the top. I do hope that you don't now slip from popularity."

"Why should she slip from popularity?" demanded the Duchess, glancing sharply at her niece. "Eleanor is too firmly established to fall from favour now."

"Yes, Aunt Lucy," returned Beatrix meekly. "It was just that I was anxious for my cousin. She's been enjoying her position as Number One debutante of the Season, and I would think it the horridest thing were she to fall into total obscurity."

"As I have said, there is no possibility of that!" The Dowager was not in the best of tempers, and Eleanor was glad that his lordship was not here, for if he had been present he would have received the lash of his aunt's tongue.

"Dearest Eleanor," Beatrix was saying half an hour later when, having knocked on the door of her cousin's bed-chamber, she was invited to enter, "do tell me all about it. I was so amazed when you returned as quickly as you did. Was it a lover's quarrel?"

Eleanor looked uncomfortable, as well she might.

"Certainly not! I've already told you, the Marquis would not even look at anyone like me – not in that way!"

"But you would like it above all things if he did?" Beatrix's voice was soft, her eyes intent.

"I shall not discuss his lordship with you, Beatrix!"

"Oh, well, there is no need to be so horrid about it," complained her cousin in high dudgeon. "I intended only to show sympathy, Eleanor!"

"I'm sorry, Beatrix, but I am not in need of your sympathy!"

"I think you have fallen in love with the Marquis," persisted Beatrix, appearing to derive considerable satisfaction from Eleanor's obvious discomfort. "I did warn you, *dearest* Eleanor, but you haven't taken heed, that's for sure. You had warning also that he was merely flirting with you, and yet you have allowed yourself to have a *tendre* for him. I consider that you've been very foolish – and that is not a bit like you, not ordinarily. Mama has so often set you up as an example to me, declaring you have more commonsense in your little finger than I have in the whole of my body. But you must admit that I have shown a great deal of wisdom since coming to London. I haven't given my heart to anyone yet!"

Listening impatiently to all this, Eleanor had the greatest difficulty in refraining from repeating what the Marquis had said about Beatrix having earned for herself the name

Coquette. However, her manners having been well learned both from her Mama and Papa, she did refrain, and even when Beatrix predicted a swift decline in her popularity, Eleanor still managed to keep a curb on her tongue.

"I know that my Aunt Lucy is confident of your remaining the rage," continued Beatrix who – Eleanor strongly suspected – was thoroughly enjoying herself, "but even she can be wrong. I cannot help feeling that, once it's generally known that the Marquis has lost interest in you, then your popularity must wane . . ." Beatrix's voice trailed off as she caught sight of the bouquet of flowers standing prettily in a cut-glass bowl which Eva had taken from the dining-room. "What a charming posy," commented Beatrix, moving over to finger one of the petals. "Where did you get it?"

And because she was only human, Eleanor drew herself up proudly and said,

"His lordship the Earl of Brockheath sent it to me today. His card is there if you would like to read it."

"The Earl of – of Brockheath," stammered Beatrix, taken aback by this astounding piece of information. "But – but it is well known that he has declared he would send flowers only to the lady he wants to marry."

Eleanor smiled quite casually and answered,

"Yes, I believe so. Am I not fortunate in bringing to myself the attention of so exalted a gentleman?" And because she was most anxious to give the lie to Beatrix's statement that she had fallen in love with the Marquis, Eleanor went on to add, "So you see now why I have not given my heart to his lordship. Wouldn't you yourself prefer a future Duke to a mere Marquis?"

Beatrix, she noticed, had turned a trifle pale.

"Yes – yes, of course I would." Stupefied now, Beatrix fell silent for a space. "Oh, but I never thought that *you* would even have such an opportunity! I don't know what my Mama will say to me, for I am sure *I* cannot win the heir to a *Dukedom*!"

Feeling by now totally overwhelmed by guilt, Eleanor wished fervently that she could undo what she had done; she thought of her Papa, knew he would be both shocked and pained at her conduct, for this was deceit of the most appalling character, and in addition employed for the sole purpose of getting her own back on her cousin – the cousin whom she had to thank for being in London at all.

"Beatrix," she began in agitated tones, "I didn't really –"

"Don't say another word, I beg of you!" cried her cousin, precariously close to a fit of the vapours. "Oh, but I wish I had never insisted on your coming her with me! For I'm sure I haven't required your company – not on one single occasion. I don't know how you could have done such an odious thing to me – encouraging the heir to a Dukedom, when I haven't managed to win one offer yet! No, do not try to interrupt me," she snapped as Eleanor held forth her hands appealingly. "I have no wish to hear anything from you – not now or ever again!" and, tears of mortification streaming down her face, Beatrix ran out of the room. "What will Mama say! Oh, but she won't be able to believe that you have outshone me . . ." Eleanor heard no more as, having reached the end of the corridor, Beatrix entered her bedchamber and slammed the door behind her.

CHAPTER
EIGHT

ALTHOUGH she would have very much liked to make a full confession to her cousin, Eleanor held back for two reasons. Firstly, Beatrix was so angry with her that it was exceedingly doubtful if she would listen, since if Eleanor only opened her mouth to speak to her she turned away. The second reason was that with Beatrix's bitter denunciation still ringing in her ears, Eleanor was herself so angry that she knew she would have difficulty in humbling herself before her cousin. Consequently, the truth never came out and Beatrix remained under the illusion that it was only a matter of time – and a short time, in all probability – before the Earl offered for her cousin. Eleanor could well understand her chagrin. As for the woman who had been the cause of it all – well, she was so filled with triumph that she seemed to shake off at least ten years of her age, and her nephew, calling at Cavendish Square the day following the visit to the theatre, remarked on this and inquired the cause of it.

"You haven't been taking any of those youth-giving elixirs I've seen advertised in the magazines?" he said, laughing.

Ignoring this, she asked him where he had been since the last time he had taken Eleanor out driving.

"I've been to Kent," was all he said, his eyes moving towards the sofa on which Eleanor was sitting.

"Kent, eh," mused the Duchess thoughtfully. "And in the height of the Season too. Now what would you be

wanting to visit your estates for at this time of the year?"
But she did not wait for an answer and she went on to tell
him she had been wanting to see him. "I am curious to
know why you and this child here have quarrelled?" she
ended, and Eleanor rose from the sofa, her voice protesting
as she said,

"Ma'am, you must know that I cannot remain if you
are to discuss me with his lordship."

The Dowager nodded.

"You may go, then, my dear," she said pleasantly. "Take
a stroll in the garden with Beatrix."

"Yes, ma'am." So her Grace had not yet noticed the
rift that had occurred between Beatrix and herself, thought
Eleanor, feeling relieved at the old lady's ignorance. Knowing
her Grace, Eleanor had for some days been expecting her to
question both her and Beatrix about their coolness
towards one another.

Quite naturally Eleanor did not seek out her cousin on
leaving the drawing-room, but went into the garden alone,
and sat under a tree which had been furnished with a
circular bench around its trunk. The sun was shining
from a clear blue sky, and in the flower borders insects
buzzed and hummed, the only sounds breaking the tranquil
silence. Within Eleanor's heart there was no tranquillity,
for she was plagued by the expectancy of an offer from
the Earl of Brockheath. His lordship would of course have
to approach the Duchess first, and then travel up to Yorkshire to see her father. But as Eleanor had no intention
of accepting him, all this would be a waste of time. She
had hesitantly mentioned her agitations to the Duchess,
but as that lady was keenly desirous of the Earl's offering
for Eleanor, her protégée received no satisfaction whatsoever from her.

"He hasn't offered yet," her Grace pointed out reason-
ably, "and, therefore, there is nothing we can do."

"I cannot accept him," Eleanor had said, but as this was dismissed with a careless flick of the Duchess's hand, Eleanor made no further attempts to enlist her help. She just waited, her apprehension growing with each day that passed, yet at the same time she would – at the end of each day – breathe a sigh of relief and tell herself that the Earl had changed his mind. The trouble was that with the return of daylight all her anxieties would begin again.

"You're looking pale, Miss," Eva had more than once remarked. "It's all this dancing and theatre-going that's beginning to tell on you. In my opinion, Miss, you ought to take a short sojourn in the country."

"I'd very much like to go home," Eleanor said, but to herself. It had been so exciting at first, coming to London for the Season; and it was no use pretending that her phenomenal rise to the top had not afforded her the utmost pleasure. A Nobody, and a provincial ... becoming the rage. Yes, it had been exceedingly gratifying, even though it would never have happened had it not been for the Dowager's almost fiendish desire to be revenged on her enemy, Lady Tiernay.

Eleanor's chief worry, though, was her own attitude towards the Marquis. It was no use denying that she had more than a *tendre* for him. In fact, she was madly in love with him. And as he was as unattainable as the stars, it was no wonder she was so unhappy, no wonder she felt she would be better at home where, if she were sensible and threw herself into the various tasks about the house, she would soon begin to forget him. As things were, she was bound to keep meeting him, even though he had – so she believed – lost interest in her.

In the midst of this brooding she glanced up – to see the object of her thoughts standing some way off, looking in her direction. She was determined to retain her composure. He should *not* put her out of countenance, she decided firmly as, looking directly at him, she somehow managed a careless smile.

"May I join you, ma'am?" His lordship's tone was brusque, his face an expressionless mask.

Eleanor adopted an air of surprise, even though, with her keen intelligence, she suddenly guessed why he was here.

"But of course, my lord. Isn't it a beautiful day? So warm and pleasant out here in the garden."

He made no reply, but sat down beside her on the bench. She cast him a glance from beneath her long dark lashes and as he seemed not to notice she had an opportunity of studying his strong features for a few moments in silence. He was far different from his friend Mr Brummell, the King of Fashion, in that he possessed tremendous strength of character in every line of his face. The jaw in profile portrayed determination, the mouth firmness and implacability. Eleanor, surveying him now as the man she loved, no longer saw anything of the dandy in him; on the contrary, she regarded him as a gentleman faultless in every way.

He turned his head at last and said, still in the same brusque tone,

"Would you come driving with me tomorrow, Miss Sherburn?"

She had known something like this was bound to come, and as she considered it best for her own peace of mind that he and she should discontinue driving together, she made no pretence as she said,

"The Duchess requested you to invite me, my lord, but as your offer is being made under pressure, I am declining it."

His eyes widened.

"That's plain speaking indeed, Miss Sherburn!"

"Haven't you and I always spoken plainly to one another?" she enquired.

"Too plainly for mere acquaintances," he murmured, in so low a tone that she almost missed his words altogether. She made no comment, feeling sure he would not wish her to do so. His next statement was made in a raised voice edged with anger. "As for your assertion, ma'am, that I act under pressure from my aunt – I think you know me well enough by now to be sure that it is not possible for anyone to put me under pressure!" His dark blue eyes were arrogant as they looked into hers; his mouth was tightly set.

"If this is so, my lord, then why are you inviting me to drive out with you?"

"Because I shall enjoy your company, Miss Sherburn," was his instant reply – and this certainly did put her out of countenance.

"But – but, s-sir, you have not wanted my – my company during these past few days?" Her voice was questioning, her lovely eyes bewildered. Was it possible that his lordship was attracted to her?

"I believe you heard me tell her Grace that I had been to Kent," he said, and now his voice was far more affable. His eyes lingered on her face, taking in the expression of doubt and uncertainty in her eyes. "I had some business to attend to there."

"I see." A smile fluttered to her lips. She forgot all her resolve about not accepting his invitation to drive out with him as she added, with a most attractive sort of hesitancy, "In that case, my lord, I shall be most happy for you to take me driving."

"Tomorrow, then?" he said, his firm mouth relaxing. "I shall take you to Hyde Park, and then, in the evening, we shall go – along with the Duchess and your cousin – to Vauxhall Gardens to see the fireworks."

She opened her eyes wide at this added offer; the Marquis smiled at her surprise but made no comment, and after remaining just a few more minutes he stood up, bowed over her hand, and took his leave of her.

Meanwhile, Beatrix, having been at the window of her bedchamber when his lordship went into the garden to seek out Eleanor, was becoming so curious to know what was happening between the Marquis and her cousin, that she found herself unable to maintain the sulky silence she invariably assumed whenever she and her cousin came into one another's company. And she surprised Eleanor by asking outright whether she and the Marquis had made up their quarrel.

"We did not have a quarrel," returned Eleanor, her voice distinctly cool, for she could not so easily forget all that her cousin had said to her, as well as having ignored her for the past few days.

"Differences, then. Have you two solved them?"

Eleanor looked curiously at her.

"Why should you be so interested?" she wanted to know.

Beatrix shrugged her shoulders in a gesture of indifference.

"I was only trying to be helpful," she replied, "but if you're going to be so odious with me —"

"I am not odious, Beatrix," broke in her cousin with some asperity. "You seem to forget that secretly you have adopted a most unfriendly attitude towards me."

"It was your own fault," said her cousin with a pout.

"I have done nothing to offend you!"

"So you think. But what am I to say to Mama if it transpires that the Earl of Brockheath offers for you?"

"As his offering for me is the most unlikely circumstance imaginable, we need not talk about it."

Beatrix frowned and changed the subject, reverting to his lordship's recent visit.

"As regards the Marquis, Eleanor, I have just mentioned

that I want to be helpful. If he is affording you his attention again, then it is only because he wants to flirt with you. I feel I *must* warn you of this."

For some reason Eleanor had the most staggering idea.

"Why," she asked with a strange inflection in her voice, "have you always been so interested in the Marquis?"

Instantly going red, Beatrix turned her head away.

"I have never been interested," she denied, but in such an unconvincing way that Eleanor could not possibly be deceived. So Beatrix also had a *tendre* for his lordship . . .

"Tell me," said Eleanor in a much less hostile tone, "why have you been flirting so much since coming to London? You've had many beaux, and you appeared to be enjoying yourself with every one of them."

"I'm merely having fun. Didn't my Mama say that I should have many London beaux?"

"She did, but . . ." Eleanor hesitated, aware that she could not mention the fact that Beatrix's flirtations had by no means gone unnoticed by the ton. "You know very well why you came here," Eleanor continued presently. "It was to find a wealthy husband. Yet you are not troubling to attract anyone who might be serious about you."

Beatrix turned at last, and Eleanor saw that her eyes were moist.

"I have been endeavouring to make the Marquis jealous," she confessed on a tiny sob. "But he does not even look at me –"

"That's not true," protested Eleanor, thinking that his lordship had always invited Beatrix to stand up with him at Almack's and other assemblies. "It is not very amiable of you to say a thing like that, Beatrix."

"He has never once asked me to drive in Hyde Park with him." A pause followed, but when Eleanor made no comment Beatrix looked steadily at her and asked, "Are you invited to drive with him, cousin?"

Biting her lip, Eleanor had to say yes, she was to drive with him the following day.

"But it means nothing," added Eleanor hastily on noting the tears that were gathering in her cousin's eyes. "You know as well as I that my situation precludes any hope of my marrying a gentleman of his lordship's standing in society. You and I have talked of this several times," she went on with a hint of impatience, "so it should be firmly fixed in your mind by now."

"What about the Earl?" Beatrix reminded her peevishly. "You're expecting an offer from him – so you implied. You said that you weren't interested in Lord Trouvaine because you could have the heir to a Dukedom, which was far better, as it suited your ambitions."

"I didn't put it quite like that," protested Eleanor indignantly. "In any case, even if the Earl did offer I couldn't accept."

"Because of your situation? Well, to tell the truth," said Beatrix outspokenly, "I don't believe he will offer once he knows your Papa is only a Vicar."

Keeping her temper with the greatest difficulty, Eleanor ignored this latter part of her cousin's speech and said quite frankly that the reason why she would have to refuse the Earl was because she had no tender feelings for him.

"You have always heard me say that I shall marry for love if my Mama and Papa will allow me to do so," she added.

"I don't believe you would refuse the Earl just because you did not love him, Eleanor."

"Then I cannot make you believe it. However, you will soon discover the sincerity of my statement, should the Earl offer for me."

"My aunt would be delighted were he to offer for you."

To this Eleanor made no response, since it was quite true. And, later in the evening when she was sitting with the Duchess in the small saloon drinking tea, Eleanor was to be questioned about her feelings for the Earl. Beatrix was out, attending a party at the home of Lady Dassett, whose son had been sent to escort her there and who would later bring her safely back to her aunt's house.

"I have no tender feelings for him at all," replied Eleanor frankly, aware of the disappointment her refusal would be for the Duchess. "In any case, ma'am, I feel that he should be given some sign that his suit will not be successful, and consequently he will refrain from making me an offer."

The Duchess was shaking her head.

"It is my desire that he shall make you an offer – even if it is refused. No, child, do not interrupt me," she added imperiously as Eleanor lifted a hand in protest. "I have my reasons for wanting him to propose marriage to you. Refuse him if you must, but if you do, in my opinion you will be very foolish indeed."

"Your Grace," said Eleanor in a low tone, "I did not come to London with the hope of making an advantageous alliance, as you very well know."

"Nevertheless, I did say, right at the start, that it was possible for you to make an advantageous alliance," the Duchess reminded her calmly. "In the past, my child, you have been too content to play second fiddle to your cousin; you were resigned to the fact that this must be so. I suspect that Beatrix's mother was more than a little to blame, for she has always doted on her daughter's beauty – which, I don't mind telling you," continued her Grace with quite disconcerting frankness, "is only superficial beauty, and not of the kind that will last. Added to this she is a muttonhead –"

"Your Grace," Eleanor broke in uncomfortably, "please, I beg of you, do not say disparaging things about my cousin. As you know, but for her I should not be here at all."

The Dowager looked shrewdly into her big brown eyes. "And so you are filled with gratitude, eh?"

"It is natural, ma'am."

"And," mused her Grace with the same shrewd glance, "I expect you are filled with gratitude towards me?"

"But of course," replied Eleanor swiftly and with one of her pretty smiles fluttering. "It must be so, mustn't it?"

"Then forget it," almost snapped her Grace. "You owe me nothing!"

A small pause followed, and then, quite unable to restrain herself, Eleanor said quietly,

"That is a strange thing to say, ma'am. Will you tell me why I should not owe you anything?"

The pale blue eyes flickered; Eleanor strongly suspected that her Grace was seriously considering telling her the truth. However, she merely shrugged and said it was of no consequence, but she did add, again employing that curt impatient tone,

"It will please me if you put all thoughts of gratitude out of your mind, Eleanor. What I have done for you was done for my own pleasure and satisfaction."

"I see." Eleanor looked penetratingly at her. "It was for your pleasure and satisfaction that you made me the rage?"

"It was." The Duchess's eyes glittered, as they had glittered on that other occasion when – so it seemed to Eleanor – she had looked positively wicked. That she was musing at this moment on her victory over her enemy was obvious by her expression, and Eleanor found herself feeling overwhelmingly thankful that the Lady Isobel really was a most odious young lady. It would have been unbearable for Eleanor had she been – as the Marquis had believed – a gentle, easy-going type of female. As it was, Eleanor felt that the Earl had had a narrow escape in not offering for her. "To get back to this question of a probable offer of marriage from the Earl of Brockheath," the Dowager was saying, "I want you to consider most carefully before you decide to refuse him. Think what an advantage such a match would be to your people. You've a brother who wants to go up to Oxford, you were telling me. Your father, too – you would be in a position to make things a little easier for him –"

"Papa would never want money from me," interrupted Eleanor swiftly. "Also, I must point out that the Earl will not offer for me once he knows of my situation."

"I've already thought of that," was the Duchess's rejoinder. "It is my intention to make you one of my beneficiaries –"

"Ma'am," Eleanor could not help saying, "this will not do! You have a son and his family; you also have the Marquis – and his ward, I believe! These should be your concern, not I!"

"The Marquis's ward was married three years ago, making one of that particular Season's most talked-of matches. The Marquis himself has no need of my money, but I shall however allow him a one-third share. One share will go to my son and the other to you." So calm her tone, and so determined her mouth. She reminded Eleanor of the Marquis when in one of his most imperious moods.

"I cannot take this," began Eleanor in some distress. "Beatrix . . .?"

"Does not require any assistance from me, " interposed her Grace even before Eleanor had finished speaking. "In any case, I would never leave anything of mine to *that* branch of the family."

Still considerably distressed, Eleanor reiterated that she was quite unable to accept what the Duchess was offering.

"It wouldn't be the thing, your Grace. Also, what about my pride?" she thought to add, but her Grace merely laughed in response to this.

"Fustian! Who cares about pride when there's a fortune at stake? As for not wanting the inheritance – well, you can't really help yourself, since I shall make my will as I wish to make it. You are distantly related to me," she thought to add.

"You are doing this solely in order that the Earl will offer for me," said Eleanor, and it was a statement, not a question. "You are intending to let it be known that I am your heiress?"

"Exactly."

"But it won't do!" cried Eleanor, becoming rather angry now. "I believe I have a right to say something, your Grace!"

"Of course. But I know what you are about to say. You are not in love with the Earl? However, from something hinted to me by Beatrix, you have promised your Mama that, on your return home, you will consider one or other of the young gentlemen who, having shown some interest in you, will need little encouragement to make you an offer. Well, my child, it would appear by this that you are not intending to marry for love."

"I want to, ma'am," cried Eleanor. "My parents married for love, and so did my sister. I have always cherished the hope that I myself might be as fortunate."

The Duchess gave a small impatient sigh.

"In your situation marriage is more important than love. I feel that you are not in a position to dally too long. You could be left behind, remember."

Eleanor nodded her head.

"Yes, ma'am, I am acutely aware of that possibility."

"Then why not accept the Earl, child? It will solve all your problems."

"He hasn't offered," began Eleanor, feeling herself being drawn into a trap of her Grace's making. It was plain that the Duchess cared not one jot for Eleanor's feelings, her sole object being to squeeze out the last ounce of satisfaction from her revenge.

At length the Duchess did drop the subject, however, but she left Eleanor pondering most seriously on the advice she had given her. The Marquis could never be hers, this Eleanor knew. Even had he not been a confirmed bachelor he would never have looked at her – seeing that he could take his pick from a hundred or more beautiful young ladies. The Earl, though appearing to be hesitating, would most likely offer for her hand in marriage. He was wealthy; as the Dowager said, marriage to him would solve all her problems. And if she wasn't going to be fortunate enough to marry for love – and she could not be now, having given her heart to the Marquis – she might as well accept the Earl. Yes, she decided, all that the Duchess said made sense. And yet . . .

"Oh, why did I have to meet his lordship!" she asked herself, by no means for the first time. "If only I had not done so, then I could have considered marriage more objectively."

She was still going over her Grace's advice when the butler announced his lordship. The Duchess, glancing at the clock, frowned at first and began to shake her head. However, she told the butler to send the Marquis up. Eleanor, with racing heart and very mixed feelings, was one moment wishing the Duchess had sent his lordship away, with the message that a quarter past ten at night was far too late an hour for him to call, and the next minute staring at the door with a mingling of pleasure and anticipation in her lovely eyes.

"What brings you here at a time like this, Justin?" the Dowager wanted to know. "It isn't like you to be on your way home at such an early hour." She stopped, her eyes taking in every detail of his immaculate attire. "Or are you on your way to one of your clubs?"

"I'm on my way home," he informed her, looking at Eleanor. Her face was delicately pink in the most enchanting way, and her dark curls were attractively awry. The Marquis's blue eyes had the most odd expression; the fingers playing with the riband of his quizzing glass tightened on it suddenly, and became still. "I thought I'd drop in to say good night."

"Mighty attentive of you," was his aunt's rather caustic rejoinder. "And since when have you considered it necessary to drop in just to bid me good night?" Her eyes, following his, were narrowed and alert. She said, in the softest of tones, "You are sure it is me you've dropped in to see?"

His mouth curved, and a shrewdness entered his eyes as he turned his attention to his aunt.

"Now what am I supposed to infer from that remark?"

"Ma'am," interrupted Eleanor, beginning to rise to her feet, "shall I leave you to converse with his lordship privately?"

The Marquis's lips twitched; Eleanor had a shrewd suspicion that he knew she wanted to escape before his aunt said anything to embarrass her.

"No, child. Sit down and drink your tea. Justin – tea for you?"

He nodded his head and sat down, on the high-backed chair opposite to Eleanor, his eyes on her face the whole time.

"I asked you what I am supposed to infer from that drily-spoken remark you have just made," said his lordship. "It would appear that you doubt my good intentions in calling on you?"

Her Grace, in the act of pouring his tea, cast him a deprecating glance.

"Why did you come?" she asked bluntly, ignoring his question.

His eyes turned again to Eleanor. She could not meet his gaze, as her heart was beating far too quickly for her comfort. The Marquis was acting most oddly indeed, and again she wondered if it were possible that he cared for her. Or was he flirting, just as Beatrix had always maintained? He himself had all but admitted this was so, on the occasion when Beatrix had eavesdropped on the conversation between the Duchess and himself.

Her Grace was holding out his tea and he rose from his chair to take it from her.

"I really did come here tonight to talk with you," he told his aunt. "And as what I have to say is rather private, I shall have to ask Miss Sherburn to leave –" He waved a hand swiftly as once again Eleanor prepared to rise from her chair. "There's no great hurry, Miss Sherburn," he went on, and she did wonder whether a note of tenderness had crept into his voice, or whether she had merely imagined it.

The Dowager looked directly at him, and then at her lovely young protégée.

"Do you know," she said after a long, deliberate pause, "I have a very good idea what you wish to talk to me about."

The Marquis, appearing to be quite unmoved by this statement, leant back languidly in his chair and sipped his tea. And after that the three of them chatted for a while before Eleanor, not feeling totally comfortable, asked to be excused.

"Don't rush off if it is not yet your bedtime," said his lordship with a smile. "My aunt and I have all night in which to talk."

Although she had the firm impression that his lordship would welcome her remaining for a little while longer, she shook her head and said with a smile,

"I am feeling rather tired, my lord. We have been out so much during the past few weeks."

"Living every moment," he observed, his keen eyes examining her face somewhat critically. "Yes, my dear, I am of the opinion that you ought to go to bed."

At the imperious manner in which this was spoken, both the Dowager and her protégée looked at his lordship in surprise. He looked stern, thought Eleanor as, standing up, he waited in a commanding way for her to leave the apartment.

"Good night, your Grace," she murmured. "Your lordship . . ."

"Good night, my dear," he said and moved to open the door for her to pass through, which she did, her head quite in a whirl, so puzzled was she by his manner. And twice he had said "my dear". What did it mean? she was still asking herself when, after being put to bed by the cheerful Eva, she lay for a long time, wondering what it was that his lordship had to say to his aunt.

"I am sure," she whispered into her pillow, "that it concerns me in some way." But, what way? She knew she was struggling to keep from her consciousness the *one idea* that was persistently attempting to form in her mind. "I mustn't think of such a possibility even for one single second," she whispered, aware that she was trembling from head to foot. "His lordship can have his pick from the richest and loveliest in the land, so it's not conceivable that he would choose me – no, not a female with no expectations, a Nobody and a provincial. In any case, he's a confirmed bachelor, everybody knows that!"

CHAPTER
NINE

THE following morning Eleanor was awake long before the arrival of Eva to draw the window blinds.

"Oh, Miss," exclaimed that cheerful young lady, "you're wide awake! Have you not had a good night?"

"It wasn't too good," confessed Eleanor. "I believe I was over-tired."

"Too many social engagements, Miss. All the young ladies making their debuts are the same; they try to fit too much in. As I was saying the other day, Miss, you could do with a sojourn in the country."

"I'm sure you are right, Eva, but it isn't possible for me to do that."

"It might be, Miss," said the maid confidingly. She drew closer to the bed. "Her Grace has just told me that the Marquis has invited her to his home in Kent. It is a certainty, Miss, that if she accepts she will take you and Miss Beatrix with her, since it could not be otherwise, could it?"

"No," murmured Eleanor in a dazed little voice. To go to the Marquis's lovely mansion in Kent . . .

"I think this dainty sprigged muslin, Miss," Eva was saying when, having bathed and put on her clean underwear, Eleanor herself was going through one of the two wardrobes in her bedchamber, undecided what to wear. "It is so becoming, making you look about sixteen, Miss, if you don't mind my saying so?"

Eleanor grimaced.

"I don't want to look as young as that, Eva!"

"Well, Miss, you never look much above seventeen. You have such a beautiful skin, and such bright eyes. And also, you wear your clothes with such an air of decorum. I don't mind saying, Miss, that your cousin's taste is not at all the thing, since it isn't *convenable* for a young girl to wear such dazzling gowns."

"Oh, but I can't have you disparage Miss Beatrix, Eva. Her Mama chose most of her gowns, and back at home in Yorkshire Lady Doynsby has a reputation for excellent taste."

"I've worked for her Grace a long while," said Eva seriously, "and during that time I have waited on numerous guests, both here and at her Grace's country mansion. And so I believe I am in a position to judge a lady's clothes. Very young girls should not aspire to emulate young matrons who are in their middle and late twenties, Miss."

Deciding not to continue with this subject, Eleanor put on the gown of sprigged muslin and then sat down, so that the maid could put the finishing touches to her hair. It was done this time in a simple style to suit the dress.

"You look very sweet, Miss. Oh, but it's such a pleasure to dress these dark locks!"

"Eva," admonished Eleanor, but with a hint of laughter in her voice, "you are the greatest flatterer I have ever met!"

"No, Miss," came the demure rejoinder, "I speak only the truth."

On entering the drawing-room some time later Eleanor was greeted rather strangely by her Grace. This lady smiled as usual, and enquired how Eleanor had slept, but all the time there was an unfathomable expression on her face — as if she were both pleased and annoyed, all at one and the same time!

"You look extraordinarily pretty today," her Grace

remarked at last. "The Marquis will obviously enjoy having such a charming female sitting beside him in his curricle."

"Thank you, ma'am." Eleanor was shy and unsure of herself all at once, because she was thinking about last night, and the Marquis's unexpected visit. "It is kind of you to say so."

The old lady laughed.

"Damme, if I oughtn't to be glad! And yet, here I am, not knowing what I want –" She stopped, her eyes twinkling as they beheld the bewildered gaze of her protégée. "I have some information for you, my child," she said, changing both her voice and her manner. "My nephew has invited me to spend a few days at Trouvaine Hall, his ancestral home in Kent. I have not quite made up my mind yet, but I rather think that both you girls would benefit from a rest. If I do decide to accept his invitation, you will both accompany me, of course."

Eleanor looked at her.

"You are in some doubt about accepting, ma'am?" She was really asking the reason for this doubt but she could scarcely ask outright. The Dowager, however, readily obliged her by saying,

"I do not want you to be away if the Earl is intending to offer for you."

Eleanor shook her head vigorously.

"I do not desire that he shall offer for me, ma'am; you are fully aware of this."

The Duchess gave a deep sigh and at the same time frowned heavily.

"I would wish him to offer, Eleanor. Then, if you really feel you must, you can refuse him. In fact, it will be well if you refuse him," she said, so suddenly and unexpectedly that Eleanor was startled.

"You do not mind if I refuse him, then?"

"I have now decided that it will please me if you refuse

him," was her Grace's bland and rather staggering reply. But, as she pondered this change, Eleanor thought she had the answer. Her Grace could see that it would be far more mortifying for Lady Tiernay if, having been refused by her Grace's protégée, the Earl should then offer for the Lady Isobel.

It was all a most dastardly and reprehensible plot, thought Eleanor with a sudden frown – and yet she could understand the Duchess's desire for revenge, seeing that she had lost her lovely young daughter through the malevolence of Lady Tiernay.

"Do you think you would like to have a short stay at the Marquis's home?" The Duchess's soft voice cutting into her reflections, Eleanor glanced at her, a swift smile leaping to her mouth.

"Yes, indeed!" she exclaimed. "Without wishing to appear ungrateful, ma'am, the social round has been more than a little exhausting. It would be the pleasantest thing if we could just live a leisurely life for a short while –" She stopped on noting the Duchess's eyes were staring over her shoulder. Twisting around, Eleanor was quite put out of countenance on meeting the steady gaze of the Marquis.

"So you are tiring of this headlong pursuit of pleasure, Miss Sherburn?" His lordship came slowly towards her. She had been about to pick up the pretty bonnet which she had brought down with her and placed on a chair, but she stepped back, in a little gesture which was almost of fear. His lordship stopped, a slight frown settling on his aristocratic brow. "Is something wrong?" he enquired. "I haven't got the plague, my dear."

To her own surprise she managed to laugh, and a dimple peeped; the Marquis's blue eyes became appreciative and intent.

"I'm sorry, my lord," said Eleanor, recovering her composure almost immediately. "I was about to put on my bonnet." There had been an unmistakable note of tenderness when he had said "my dear", and suddenly her heart was singing.

"Then allow me," rejoined the Marquis, picking up the bonnet and again advancing towards her. This time she remained still, and merely looked up at him as, having put on her bonnet, he proceeded to tie the ribbons under her left ear. "Very charming," he murmured . . . and by some subtle manoeuvre his lips happened to be very close to her cheek. She blushed and lowered her eyes, her long dark lashes fluttering under his gaze.

"A pretty picture," remarked the Duchess with the merest hint of satire. "I do believe you're becoming human, Justin."

Eleanor's colour fluctuated, and a lovely smile hovered on her lips.

"If you're ready, my child," said his lordship, ignoring his aunt's comment, "we'll be on our way."

A few minutes later, Eleanor was sitting beside him as he drove his magnificent pair of greys along the road. She waited with a mixture of anxious expectancy for his lordship to speak. She thought for one wild moment that he might come right out and propose marriage to her, while the next she was telling herself sternly that she was adopting a far too confident attitude. Also, even if he were courting her in earnest, he would never offer for her without first approaching her father. Nevertheless, she felt confident that he had, last night, discussed her with the Duchess; this was revealed by her Grace's manner – for she had evinced no surprise whatsoever when his lordship, in that proprietorial way, had taken up Eleanor's bonnet and proceeded to put it on and tie the ribbons for her.

"Are you quite comfortable?" inquired his lordship, breaking the silence at last. "Is the sun in your eyes?"

She shook her head.

"No, my lord; I am perfectly comfortable."

"And happy?" murmured his lordship softly.

"Yes – er – of c-course."

Turning his head, he regarded her with some amusement.

"You're shy all at once. Surely you are not losing that most attractive *hardiesse* with which I have become more than a little familiar?"

She laughed then, and retorted,

"If I am ever impudent with you, sir, it is because you have given me provocation!"

"That's better! Do we spar again ... or chat on more congenial lines?"

"It is up to you, my lord!"

"Very well; we shall call a truce."

"You're absurd," she laughed. "We have never really *fought*."

"Not yet ... but there is time." He glanced across the road to where a very dashing young female was driving herself in a high-perch phaeton. "The wealthy Miss Cobham," he explained as Eleanor followed the direction of his gaze. "A young lady of *her* means is allowed to have her whims, and driving herself about is one of them. It's a wonder you haven't seen her shopping in Bond Street?"

Eleanor shook her head. She just had to ask,

"Do you know her well, sir?"

"If you mean, are we closely acquainted, the answer's no. We have so little in common, you see." His voice was a trifle stiff and contemptuous.

"You do not approve of females driving themselves about, my lord?"

"I'm indifferent to what the regular run of females do. I would not allow my wife to drive out on her own." This sentence was uttered in a masterful tone of voice which had suddenly become quite stern. Eleanor was fast learning that the foppish exterior she had once seen was no more than a thin veneer covering admirable traits which were having a profound effect upon her, traits which she found exceedingly attractive. She dwelt for a long while on his mention of the word "wife", recalling all that had been said of him – the confident assertions that he would never marry. Eva had maintained that his reason for remaining single was that he preferred opera-dancers, that he would never be able to settle down to *one*.

"I conclude that my aunt has informed you of the invitation I've made for a visit to my home in Kent?"

"Yes," replied Eleanor, all eagerness. "Her Grace tells me that, should she decide to accept, then Beatrix and I shall come also?"

"Correct."

"You heard me telling her Grace that I would enjoy the rest above all things."

"I did." His eyes wandered again, to a rather grand barouche drawn by a pair of high stepping chestnuts. This equipage drew a great deal of attention from the Fashionable Parade seen in Hyde Park at this hour during the Season, since it belonged to one of the Duke of Cumberland's lights o' love. Casting his lordship a sideways glance, she could not miss the half sneering, half sardonic smile that had risen to his lips. "I think you will be able to have all the rest you desire," he assured her, returning his attention to the topic under discussion. "We lead a most sequestered existence at Trouvaine."

"You go there often?" she asked in some surprise.

His dark eyes regarded her quizzically.

"I believe you have formed a rather warped impression of me my dear," he said.

Her heart quickened because of the gently-spoken "my dear", and because of the unmistakable expression of tenderness in his eyes.

"I must admit," she returned with incurable honesty,

"that I have gained the impression that you are quite happy in your role of Arbiter of Fashion and Leader of Society."

The Marquis frowned darkly, which was designed to put her out of countenance. However, having heard of his famous set-downs – and in fact having more than once herself come very near to being the target for one of them – she decided to adopt an armour which he would have difficulty in penetrating, and she was all cool composure as she awaited his response to what she had said to him. The frown remained for a space and then he laughed, a little to her surprise ... and a great deal to her delight. For as she'd noticed before, he was alarmingly attractive when he laughed, fine wrinkles fanning out at the corners of his eyes and mouth. Eleanor, living as she was increasingly in a cloud of heady dreams, felt her pulse increase in time with the uncontrollable racing on of her thoughts – to an exciting future as the wife of his lordship.

"I am fast coming to the conclusion," remarked my lord in a very soft tone, "that a beating would do you the world of good."

"Oh ... my lord!" She certainly was put out now – and it suddenly dawned on her that although his lordship had laughed, his intention to give her a set-down had remained. And he had succeeded – much to her chagrin. "What an indelicate thing to say to a female!"

"Don't be missish," he laughed. "It isn't as if you're not used to my particular manner of speaking."

"I am of the firm opinion," said Eleanor with a mingling of dignity and accusation, "that you would not speak so to *any* female. It is just me whom you treat differently!"

The dark blue eyes surveyed her tilted profile thoughtfully.

"So you've taken umbrage," he observed with cool unconcern.

"Is it not understandable, sir?"

He said, after some seconds of thoughtful silence,

"Has it not occurred to you, my child, that there must be a strong reason for my treating you differently?"

She turned her head so swiftly that a dark curl swung round and touched his cheek.

"My – my lord ...?" she murmured, aware that her cheeks were glowing. "What d-do y-you mean?"

Again he laughed.

"How refreshing you are!" He stopped to lift a careless hand in response to a greeting sent to him by a fellow member of the Bow-window Set, the Honourable Josiah Tolworth, another Arbiter of Fashion and Taste. "It so happens," resumed his lordship as he drove on through the Park, "that I treat you differently because you are different."

This was flattery pure and simple; no damsel, however slow-witted, could fail to grasp the implication of words like those, especially as they were uttered in tones both of gentleness and sincerity.

"I do not know what to say, my lord," she murmured at last, lowering her long lashes in order to conceal her expression, for his lordship's head was turned towards her and he was scrutinising her both with amusement and admiration.

"You mean," he just had to say, "that for once you are tongue-tied?"

"My lord, you are the most odious person!"

"I sincerely hope that you are not serious, ma'am," he rejoined with mock concern. "You see, it is my greatest desire that I may find favour in your eyes."

Blushing hotly at this near-proposal of marriage, she was in fact completely speechless, which was to be expected, of course, seeing that something beyond her wildest dreams was happening. She was not only to make a brilliant match but, far more important, she was to marry for love. It was a miracle, and even though in her heart of hearts she was fully convinced that his lordship meant to offer for her, there was a tiny bit of her that could not believe what was really happening. "My dear," the Marquis was saying, "allow me to remind you of your manners. His Grace the Duke of Leicester has just made you a bow – No, this side. He is riding the chestnut stallion. Ah, and here comes your friend and mine – George! I had better rein in and we can exchange civilities for a moment or two. It will also give the horses a rest," he added, half-turning to his tiger. "Perhaps you would care to stroll for a while – after we have conversed with our friend?" he added and, when Eleanor said yes, she would enjoy that above all things, he instructed the tiger to take the horses' heads.

George Brummell, always a familiar participant in the Fashionable Promenade of riders, drivers and pedestrians to be found between the hours of five and six – weather permitting – in Hyde Park in the height of the Season, also stopped, and the three chatted for five minutes or so. Many heads turned, and Eleanor could not but feel a certain degree of elation to be standing here, conversing with the two most important Corinthians, both attired in the latest style of elegance, both affording her that sort of attention which must, without any doubt at all, raise her consequence to an even higher level than it had already reached. And then, as if this were not enough, who should ride up but the Earl of Brockheath, who also stopped for a chat. His eyes, scarcely ever leaving Eleanor's face, revealed all the admiration he felt for her, and the Marquis, noting this undisguised interest, began to treat the Earl with what could only be described as icy politeness, endeavouring to bring the discourse to a speedy conclusion. However, as the Beau and the Earl began to discuss Bruiser Brownlow, a prizefighter whose victories were winning for him the admiration of all who visited the Parlour where the bouts took place, the Marquis perforce had to listen, while Eleanor amused herself by watching the passers-by – the Dowagers in their crested barouches, the young sprigs of fashion in their curricles or riding on horseback, the fashionable Mamas with their doe-eyed daughters – all were on parade on this sunny afternoon, and all would later be attending the various entertainments that were provided for their pleasure.

Suddenly, who should appear in her carriage but the Lady Isobel, with her grandmother beside her. And as they drove quite close to where the three men and Eleanor were standing, Eleanor was able to note Lady Tiernay's malevolent scowl. Isobel, equally vicious in expression, added her own baleful glance to that of her grandmother, and unable to bear it, Eleanor turned away so abruptly that all three of her companions looked at her, surprised. She made no comment, naturally, and the three men in turn made their salutations to the two titled ladies as they passed on their way towards the gate through which the carriage was seen to pass.

Looking at the Earl, Eleanor saw him give a small shrug of his shoulders, as if, aware that he was out of favour in that particular quarter, he was telling himself that it was of no consequence.

The weather remained warm throughout the evening, and both Eleanor and her cousin decided to wear light gowns, with opera cloaks of taffeta over them, for the party at Vauxhall Gardens. They had been on several occasions before, but the many thousands of lamps, hanging in festoons reaching from one colonnade to another, never failed to bring gasps of delight to their lips. These lamps illuminated the gardens in the most attractive way, but even so there were numerous dark, secluded places where lovers could stroll without being seen. In a huge kiosk, lit

by multi-coloured lamps, was the orchestra, while another
attraction was the Pavilion, its many mirrors glittering like
something out of fairyland. It was the main supper parlour,
used by people who preferred not to go to the expense of
hiring one of the private boxes. Yet another attraction was
the Rotunda where, in the Season, concerts were held.
Fountains and beautifully laid-out groves added to the
splendour.

The Marquis met them and conducted them for a short
stroll along one of the colonnaded walks to the Rotunda,
where they watched a scene of medieval activity most
cleverly portrayed, before sauntering to the box he had
booked. Here they partook of supper while listening to the
orchestra and watching the pageant of fashionable society
as it passed in a never-ending stream before their box. Mr.
Brummell stopped for a word before strolling away to join
the Earl of Sutherby and his betrothed, the Lady Catherine
Granville; the Marquis of Linross and his wife stopped
for a word or two as they made their way to the Grand
Cascade.

"I must admit," declared Beatrix as she selected a thin
slice of ham from the plate in front of her, "that I am very
taken up with London life!"

Casting her a glance, Eleanor could not help reflecting
on her infatuation for Hugh Sommerville, and thinking
that it had not taken her very long to get over it.

The Duchess was regarding her niece with a hint of
disapproval.

"You appear to have forgotten why you came to London," she said bluntly. "This flirting won't do. If you're
not careful you'll be going home without having attained
your object – and that won't please your Mama," her Grace
could not help adding. But if she expected to set her niece
to the blush she was mistaken. Beatrix merely shrugged her
shoulders and said,

"Can I help it, Aunt Lucy, if all the young gentlemen find me attractive?" and she cast a sideways glance at his lordship. Eleanor, who happened to catch the glance, saw that Beatrix still had an interest in the Marquis. What was she going to say when she learned that his lordship had offered for her cousin? wondered Eleanor, frowning in a troubled way. She did not wish to hurt Beatrix, but she could not deny that she was very much looking forward to the never-to-be-forgotten moment when his lordship did ask her to marry him. Of course, he would have to approach her father first, so she was not expecting him to make his proposal in the immediate future. These reflections led, quite naturally, to thoughts of the Earl of Brockheath, and the delay on his part. Eleanor was sure that the Duchess had expected an offer before now. She had not given up hope, though – quite the reverse, since it was owing to her expectation of an offer from the Earl that her Grace was undecided about accepting her nephew's invitation to stay at his home in Kent. It was also clear to Eleanor now, that although the Duchess had this insane desire to be revenged on her old enemy, she had no real wish that Eleanor should become the bride of the Earl. Knowing of her nephew's feelings for Eleanor, the Duchess must surely want to see him attain his desire.

"My dear ..." The Marquis's soft voice as he interrupted her reverie was like music to Eleanor's ears, so marked with tenderness did it appear to be. "Where are you, my child?"

"With my own private thoughts, my lord," she replied saucily.

Her cousin's head turned swiftly, and her eyes narrowed as they travelled from the unsmiling countenance of the Marquis, to Eleanor's sweetly-smiling face. Beatrix licked her lips, and her pretty rosebud mouth set in a tight little line.

"What were those thoughts?" his lordship demanded. "No, don't you dare tell me any fibs! I want the truth!"

"Justin," admonished his aunt, "what a way to speak to Eleanor! What reason have you for suspecting that she might tell you an untruth?"

"Past experience," replied his lordship without hesitation.

"You must have provoked me," she said.

"What were your thoughts?" he repeated, by-passing what she had just said. "They were of the most interesting, judging by your expression."

"They were private, my lord, as I have just stated."

He looked at her through eyes that had narrowed suddenly, but whatever he had intended saying died on his lips as he caught Beatrix's eyes fixed upon his face. His brows lifted a fraction in a gesture of arrogance and it was Beatrix's turn to look away. The Dowager, suddenly aware of the tension, broke in with some triviality and from then on the conversation became light and inconsequential.

When supper was finished they all watched the fireworks, the Duchess appearing to be bored, but Eleanor exclaiming now and then as some of the more astonishing set pieces unfolded before her eyes. Beatrix was also entertained, but once or twice Eleanor, trying to catch her eye, saw that she was in a rather petulant mood.

"I don't know how you can allow him to flirt with you in that odious manner," she told Eleanor severely when, after their arrival home in the early hours of the morning, she looked into her cousin's bedchamber before retiring to her own. Eva had offered to stay up to undress her mistress but Eleanor would not have it. And so she was alone when Beatrix entered the room. "And you yourself – I suppose your realize how shocked your Papa would be were he to know of your behaviour!"

"I do not flirt with his lordship," retorted Eleanor indignantly. "Nor does he flirt with me!"

The big blue eyes opened wide.

"Are you trying to convince me that the Marquis has a *tendre* for you?" enquired Beatrix scornfully. "Let me tell you, Eleanor, that you are setting your cap far too high altogether! First you're confident that the heir to a Dukedom will offer for you, and then you're expecting a Marquis to do so – and not an ordinary Marquis," almost sneered Beatrix, her eyes flashing derisively, "but a very special one – the most sought-after bachelor of them all! And one of the wealthiest gentlemen in the country." She looked her cousin over from head to foot. "You're absurd, Eleanor!" And with this parting shot, she flounced from the room.

CHAPTER
TEN

HALF expecting her cousin to be in the same disagreeable mood when they met the following morning, Eleanor was pleasantly surprised to be greeted as if nothing had happened.

"Aunt Lucy's taking us to Bond Street," Beatrix told her, her big blue eyes shining with excitement. "I must say, Eleanor, that I adore shopping in London! All those clothes are in the first rank of fashion! And the hats! I am intending to buy myself that *adorable* creation with the ostrich feathers which I was so undecided about the last time we went to Bond Street, do you remember?"

Eleanor nodded her head.

"I did say how much it suited you," she reminded Beatrix.

"I know; I should have taken your advice and bought it at the time. I do hope it hasn't been sold to someone else, for I'm sure it couldn't look as pretty on another girl as it did on me!"

Faintly amused, Eleanor agreed. But she felt she ought to mention the price.

"Thirty-eight guineas is rather a lot to pay for one hat," she grimaced. However, Beatrix dismissed this with a careless flick of her hand, saying she had plenty of money left from the large sum her Papa had given her.

"In any case," she added, "Papa will send me some more if I inform him that I'm getting short."

Although the Duchess took them to Bond Street in her

carriage, she dropped them off, then ordered her coachman to drive on. She had some business to attend to, she told the girls, adding,

"Keep together. You know by now that a respectable female is never seen alone in Bond Street."

"Yes, ma'am," returned Eleanor, but Beatrix merely tossed her lovely golden head and remarked, as soon as her aunt had gone,

"Some of the ideas here are so nonsensical as to be laughable. Why shouldn't we be seen on our own?"

Eleanor shrugged.

"It is just not the thing, Beatrix."

"Oh, well, never mind it! Let's go and buy that hat!"

Over an hour later, having bought the hat and much else besides, the two girls amused themselves watching other people's horses being walked up and down the street by grooms or tigers, while the owners of the carriages were in the shops, making their purchases.

"I like the bustle of the London scene!" exclaimed Beatrix. "I think I should like to live here all the time!"

Eleanor had to laugh, and to remind her cousin of her previous declaration that all she wanted was to live quietly in the country with her Hugh.

"Ah, yes, but I hadn't tasted this good life at that time," retorted Beatrix. "Now that I *have* tasted it I know that it would suit me."

"I cannot say the same, Beatrix. I find myself confused by all the invitations. I was so tired at Almack's the other night that I could have found myself a quiet seat somewhere and gone to sleep!"

It was Beatrix's turn to laugh.

"How funny you'd have looked!"

"Undoubtedly . . ." Her voice trailed away as one of Beatrix's many beaux, having noticed the two girls standing there, brought his curricle to a halt and, ordering his tiger

to go to the horses' heads, jumped down and began chatting
to the girls. His eyes, frank and smiling, scarcely ever left
Beatrix's pretty face – and when they did they merely
travelled over her dainty figure, taking in the curves, and
the elegance of her attire. Fully aware of his concentrated
attention, Beatrix flirted with him, using all her charms.
The young gentleman, Lord Teviot, was one of the Dandy
Set, and a notable whip. But he had a reputation for col-
lecting and distributing various items of gossip, with the
result that he had been nicknamed the "Babbler". So
neither girl was surprised when eventually they heard him
say,

"Have you heard about Lord Dunstanworth and Mrs.
Vane?"

No, said the girls in unison, they hadn't. At which he
went on to allege that an affair between the couple had
resulted in Lady Dunstanworth going into a decline.

"How sad," murmured Beatrix, obviously deciding some
comment should be made on this intelligence. "For myself,
I would not allow grief to overcome me to the extent where
I went into a decline."

"No?" He looked quite surprised. "You're so – fragile,
and so helpless – sort of. I should have thought that you
could be very easily hurt." As Beatrix said nothing to this
his lordship continued by saying he had known several
women who had suffered as Lady Dunstanworth was
suffering at this time. "However, I suppose the classic case
– and the most tragic – was that of your aunt's daughter –
but of course you will know all about it?"

Eleanor stiffened, fumbling for something to say that
would prevent her cousin from pursuing this subject. But
before she could speak Beatrix had said uncomprehend-
ingly,

"Aunt Lucy – the Duchess? Did she have a daughter?
She has mentioned a son, but –"

"You didn't know?" Lord Teviot broke in eagerly. "She never told you about the beautiful Catherine – and the cause of her death?"

Beatrix shook her head, rather dazedly.

"Tell me about it," she invited, sending a sideways glance at her cousin and wondering why she had turned pale.

"It was before my time, of course," began his lordship. "But my mother and grandmother sometimes talk of it. The trouble began because of some enmity between the Duchess and Lady Tiernay, who also had a beautiful daughter of marriageable age. At that time brunettes were all the rage – "

"Lord Teviot," broke in Eleanor desperately, "please do not repeat gossip. It is something I deplore . . . I'm sorry –"

"But I want to hear it," said Beatrix determinedly. "Sir, I am exceedingly interested. Please continue."

Lord Teviot appeared undecided, his eyes moving from Beatrix to Eleanor and back again.

"Well . . ." he began, when once again Beatrix said encouragingly,

"Please continue, my lord. After all, the Duchess is *my* aunt," she added with another glance in her cousin's direction, "and so it is natural that I should be interested. Eleanor, dearest, if you would be embarrassed, then pray walk to that shop window and look at the gloves."

"I will stay," returned Eleanor stiffly, but she sent the young gentleman such an imploring glance that he shook his head and said he could not possibly discuss anything that would offend a lady. And with a little bow he turned from them and within a few moments he was driving away. Beatrix turned angrily to her cousin.

"I wanted to know the story!" she snapped. "It would have helped to solve the mystery – I know it would! I told you I intended to find out what is going on and I could have done so if you hadn't interfered!" She looked at Eleanor through hard, angry eyes, taking in her pallor, her discomfort and the fact that she was avoiding Beatrix's gaze. "*You* have known all along what's going on, why my aunt should want to make you all the rage, why she should have changed the fashion from blondes to brunettes! I demand to be enlightened," she fumed. "As I said to Lord Teviot, the Duchess is *my* aunt, and I'm naturally entitled to know just what she's been about in favouring you!"

"Beatrix," pleaded Eleanor quietly, "I cannot tell you anything –"

"If it's because my aunt told you secrets, and you feel you cannot reveal these, then I assure you, Eleanor, that you can trust me implicitly not to divulge anything you might say to me in confidence." It was an invitation, but one which Eleanor did not intend to accept. In any case, were she to enlighten her cousin, she would then have to admit that she had overheard the Duchess and her nephew talking together, and this she was not prepared to do.

"Your aunt has never told me any secrets, Beatrix –"

"Yet you know what's been going on. And you needn't deny it, because your expression gave you away just now, as did your request to Lord Teviot not to continue with what he was intending to reveal to me." She looked straight at Eleanor. "I am asking you what it is you are hiding, Eleanor – and before you answer me, please remember that you are a Vicar's daughter."

At this Eleanor's eyes blazed. It was not often she lost her temper, but she was on the verge of losing it at that moment.

"Are you implying that I might tell you an untruth?" she demanded wrathfully.

"I think that you might be tempted to prevaricate."

"Well, I am not tempted to prevaricate Not any more than I am tempted to pander to your curiosity!"

Fuming, Beatrix turned from her and stared into a shop window, tapping her tiny foot on the ground.

"I shall ask my aunt what it is all about," she decided at last. "I said I meant to solve the mystery, and solve it I shall!"

However, it was Lord Teviot, after all, who enlightened Beatrix, as he was present at a party to which she had also been invited by Lady Dassett's married daughter.

And as soon as she could manage to get Eleanor on her own the next morning Beatrix informed her that she knew everything. After repeating what Lord Teviot had told her she then added,

"The rest I can guess, obviously. I consider it exceedingly odious of my aunt to embark on so shabby a plot. The Lady Isobel doesn't seem such a bad person to me, but in any case, my aunt had no right to make her pay for something which her grandmother had done!"

"I have nothing to say," returned Eleanor quietly when, after a long silence, Beatrix made several impatient little noises with her tongue.

"You wouldn't have been the rage if it hadn't been for my aunt!"

"You said at one time that you didn't resent this," was her cousin's quiet reminder.

"Well, I did resent it! Blondes were *in*! My Mama knew this, and had they stayed in I should by now have received many favourable offers. I hate my aunt!" Tears of mortification shone in her eyes, and her small hands were clenched. "It's all so unfair – and you don't seem at all troubled that I am cast in the shade!"

"I'm sorry, Beatrix." Eleanor, genuinely distressed, wished for one unhappy moment that she had never come to London ... but the next moment her heart was light, in spite of this dissension. For her thoughts had flown to the Marquis; she knew he was intending to ask her to marry him. But what would Beatrix have to say to it all? Eleanor was soon asking herself, by no means for the first time. There would be another scene, that was certain. However, for the present no more was said, as the Duchess, having just risen from her bed, entered the room.

The Marquis's stately home exceeded all Eleanor's expectations. Surrounded on every side by magnificent scenery and rich agricultural lands, Trouvaine Hall, graceful and majestic, stood on an eminence, a striking feature of the landscape. Arriving in her Grace's crested travelling-chaise, Eleanor stared with admiration at everything she saw. Passing through the lodge gates, the carriage bowled along through the deer-park, with the most picturesque scenery opening out in every direction – undulating hills and dells, valleys and streams. The history of the hall, her Grace had informed Eleanor, could be traced back to the Conquest. Scarcely anything of the original structure now remained and the present building was the product of the Renaissance when buildings were designed with symmetry and beauty being the main order of the day. It was a "venerable" hall, the Duchess had said, and she was right. Its noble owner was patron of twenty-eight livings, and Lord of the Manor of thirty-four villages.

The Marquis was there, at the front door, when the carriage at last came to a halt. With his usual courtesy he handed down her Grace, then Eleanor, and lastly, Beatrix. Several flunkeys stood around, waiting for the visitors to move inside, when they would be able to unload the trunks and bandboxes which had followed the ladies in a separate conveyance on their journey from London.

"Welcome to Trouvaine Hall." The Marquis took Eleanor's hand after assisting her cousin to alight from the chaise. He raised it to his lips, merely brushing the fingers, while his dark eyes never left her lovely face. She returned his gaze fixedly for some minutes as something in his eyes held her, fascinated, like a timid creature staring into the eyes of its predator.

But in the Marquis's eyes she saw only admiration and tenderness, and there was a softness about his mouth that made her wish – for one wild and blushing moment – that her own lips were pressed to it. Swiftly she averted her head.

Suddenly he gave a low, humorous laugh and, as if forgetting altogether that he had other guests, he put out a hand and tilted up Eleanor's face.

"Shy again," he murmured, very softly. "I wonder just how long it will last?"

Her lips quivered, and her brown eyes twinkled. She said, suddenly feeling almost childishly mischievous,

"Until you provoke me, my lord!"

At which his blue eyes glinted.

"I shall do more than provoke you, my girl, if you don't take care!"

"Justin," said her Grace with a frown that could have denoted either boredom or impatience, but which, Eleanor suspected, was merely an affectation, "do we enter these venerable portals, or must we remain here for the night?"

His laugh was infectious – at least to Eleanor. She chuckled, then laughed outright, little knowing how profoundly she was affecting his lordship, or suspecting that his heart could be beating just as rapidly as hers.

"Sorry, Aunt Lucy. But need I invite you to enter? It's not like you to stand on ceremony. If my memory serves me correctly, the last time you arrived here I was away on one of my other estates, and on my return I found you in possession, ordering the servants about and having had two of my drawing-rooms completely rearranged –"

"Not completely," she denied. "Only partly. They were altogether too severe in aspect – they shouted the word 'bachelor' at me every time I entered them. I hope you haven't returned them to their former austerity?"

Silence for a space and then,

"I had; but when I was down here recently I had them changed again."

The Duchess nodded; her pale eyes moved to where Eleanor was now standing, close to her cousin.

"For any particular reason?" she enquired sardonically.

"Of course," was his bland rejoinder. "And you know precisely what that reason is."

The glimmer of a smile touched her lips, but all she said was,

"Come, let us be shown to our bedchambers. I'm tired after the journey, and I'm sure these children are as well."

Eleanor's room was even grander than the one she occupied at Cavendish Square, being larger and more lavishly furnished. The four-poster bed, coming out from one tapestry-hung wall, was covered with an exquisitely-worked counterpane; the couch and chairs were overlaid with threads of gold and silver, and the massive chimney-piece was made of alabaster and black marble.

To Eva, who had accompanied the Duchess on previous visits to the Marquis's country estate, these grand surroundings were familiar territory. So Eleanor felt she should refrain from appearing too naive and sternly repressed the appreciative exclamation which rose involuntarily to her lips.

"I think my white satin gown – the one with the rosebuds at the waist and hem – will be suitable for dinner this evening," she was saying to the maid a short while later. "It isn't too elaborate for a dinner at home – and in the country." At home ... So unthinkingly she had said this. Eva merely smiled, and nodded her head in agreement that the gown would be suitable.

"Your hair just simple, Miss. Ringlets falling on to your

shoulders and merely tied loosely with a riband that is more ornamental than functional?"

"I shall leave my hair entirely to you, Eva," smiled Eleanor, "for I could not presume to argue with your taste."

"Thank you, Miss," returned Eva calmly. "I do not pretend that I am *not* an expert, simply because I have had so much proof that I *am*." There was nothing immodest in her voice or her manner; she was stating a fact and Eleanor could not but admire her for her frankness.

On making her appearance for dinner Eleanor had every confidence that she had never looked more attractive – not even when she had been in full dress for her presentation at Carlton House. The Marquis, himself immaculate, and in the first rank of fashion, allowed his eyes to rove over her from head to foot, taking in the firm and classical contours of her face, the limpid brown eyes set wide apart, the generous mouth and little pointed chin. Her dark tresses shone in the candlelight; one small hand came up and tugged, with a little nervous gesture, at the end of a ringlet, a movement that brought a gleam to his eyes.

"Allow me to congratulate you on your appearance, Miss Sherburn," he said softly. "You look particularly beautiful tonight."

Naturally she coloured, a smile fluttering to her lips.

"Thank you, my lord," she returned shyly, suddenly aware of Beatrix's eyes fixed intently upon her. She turned, then gasped at the expression on her cousin's face, for what she saw there was almost akin to hatred!

Despite the hurt this caused Eleanor, the evening passed most pleasantly. The culmination of her happiness was to come after they had all retired to the drawing-room. The Marquis, having somehow managed to get her to the far side of this magnificent apartment, whispered in her ear,

"I hope, my love, that this house finds favour with you ... because I am cherishing the hope that you will soon be making it your home."

She swallowed hard, her heart racing so madly that breathing actually became difficult.

"M-my l-lord ..." was all she could manage to say – and it was a great relief when the Duchess, speaking with that sardonic inflection that had been heard in her voice before, enquired of his lordship if she was to receive her glass of sherry now, or must she wait till midnight. He laughed, immediately leaving Eleanor's side and obligingly pouring out the sherry.

"For you, too?" he enquired of Eleanor, but she shook her head, saying she would have a glass of sherbet.

"Sherbet for you, Miss Doynsby?" he then asked.

"I'll have sherry," returned Beatrix shortly. "A large portion, if you please."

All three stared at her, but Eleanor alone understood, and she gave a small sigh. Beatrix was unhappy at the turn of events, for it was obvious that the Marquis was no longer flirting with Eleanor, but that he was in deadly earnest. And, with her quick intellect and infinite understanding, Eleanor knew just how disappointed her cousin must be, caring as she did for the Marquis. Not that Eleanor set much store by the strength of Beatrix's attachments. Her feelings for the Marquis were little different from those she had known for Hugh Sommerville. And time had proved that apparently deeply-felt relationship was but a mere infatuation.

"He's madly in love with you," Beatrix said later when, having come into Eleanor's bedchamber, she had sat on the couch and waited for Eva to depart. "But he doesn't know everything, does he?"

Eleanor frowned.

"What do you mean?"

"He doesn't know that you preferred the heir to a Dukedom –"

"I did not!" broke in Eleanor indignantly, thinking of the Earl of Brockheath's call at Cavendish Square a few days ago. Beatrix had been out, and Eleanor was sitting with the Duchess when the Earl was announced.

"He's come to propose!" declared her Grace, her eyes lighting up with triumph. And to the butler she had said, in a much louder tone, "Show him in, Hobbes."

The ensuing embarrassment was something Eleanor thought, at the time, she would never forget. The Earl, addressing her Grace, had confessed to being in love with Eleanor, and had asked leave to address her. Unable to cause him too much humiliation, Eleanor had immediately interrupted with the words,

"My lord, pray do not go any further! I am sorry, but I cannot return your love!"

There had been further words, mainly between the Earl and her Grace who, most deftly indeed, had managed to soothe his lordship's ruffled feelings. However, his final imploring words had been,

"I would not like it to be put on the tongues of the gossips that I offered for a lady's hand, and she refused me. Can I ask you both to keep silent about this little scene?"

Watching the Duchess, and aware that the pinnacle of her revenge on Lady Tiernay would have been to set it abroad that Lady Isobel's beau had offered for the brunette whom she had made the rage, Eleanor feared for one long moment that the Earl's very reasonable request would be refused. However, after some thought the Duchess had come to the conclusion that the Earl was far too nice a gentleman to be subjected to that kind of humiliation, and she promised that the scene just enacted would remain the secret of the three of them. And so it had never come to Beatrix's ears that her cousin had turned down one of the Season's most eligible bachelors.

"Oh, yes, you did!" cried Beatrix in answer to her cousin's vehement denial. "You told me you preferred the heir to a Dukedom! In fact, your exact words were, 'So you see now why I have not given my heart to his lordship. Wouldn't you yourself prefer a Duke to a mere Marquis?'" Beatrix's hard eyes raked her contemptuously. "You've only turned your attention to the Marquis because Lord Brockheath didn't come up to scratch, after all. I told you he wouldn't, once he knew your situation. And I might also add, Eleanor, that although it appears that the Marquis is in love with you, you'll be very lucky if he does propose. I'm sure he's a sensible gentleman, and if he will only hesitate long enough to think about your situation, he'll have second thoughts about asking you to – to m-marry h-him –" She broke off, and burst into tears. "I hate you! I was the one who came to London to make a good match! My Mama will be furious if you outshine me! I won't let you do it! I shall tell his lordship just what you said to me!" And with that she rose and advanced swiftly to the door. Starting up, Eleanor followed, catching hold of her hand as she put it out to touch the latch.

"You wouldn't harm me like that, Beatrix. Haven't we always been bosom friends? I love the Marquis –"

"You are interested only in his money and position!" broke in Beatrix with a sneer. "I never thought you were such a – a viper!"

Eleanor's eyes opened wide.

"What an odious accusation to make!"

"It's the truth! I shall repeat to his lordship what you said to me."

"I can't think you would be so unkind, and so spiteful," returned Eleanor, her face devoid of colour and her spirits sinking at the idea of her cousin's being able to shatter her whole life's happiness. "Please, I beg of you, do not tell his lordship what I said. I didn't mean it, truly I didn't – although to you at this moment it might seem that I am telling an untruth. You had been unkind to me, declaring that his lordship was only flirting with me, and you had so many times reminded me of my situation, saying no gentleman of consequence would entertain the idea of asking me to be his wife, that on your seeing the flowers sent me by the Earl, I spoke without thinking properly. I spoke in anger, Beatrix, and in retaliation –"

"Are you blaming me for what you said?"

"Yes, Beatrix, I am. But within a few moments I regretted my odious behaviour and would have confessed the truth – that I didn't care for the Earl and that I would refuse him if he did happen to offer for me – but you didn't give me time."

"I don't believe one word of what you've just said. It's nothing but fustian!"

"It's the truth," persisted Eleanor desperately. "At that time you had asserted I was in love with the Marquis, and as I naturally didn't want to own to it – believing as I did that he would never look at anyone like me – I said those things which I have since regretted." She stopped, realizing it was a waste of time to expect her cousin to relent. It was clear from Beatrix's taut mouth and hard, glittering eyes that she intended repeating to his lordship what Eleanor had said to her.

And, immediately on meeting his lordship the following morning at ten o'clock, Eleanor knew that her chance of happiness with him had indeed been shattered by her cousin. His manner was icily polite, his voice like a knife in her heart, as after greeting her, he said,

"I must request you, ma'am, to forget what I said last evening. I fear I was rather in my cups when I spoke of your making this house your home."

Pale of face, and with her beautiful eyes shadowed, Eleanor looked up at him, noting his drawn expression and the nervous movement of a vein in his throat. She just had to say,

"You've been talking to my cousin, sir?"

"I would rather not speak of it –"

"I can only apologise, my lord, for something I said on impulse, but which I did not mean. Further than that I cannot explain," she added, wishing she were not bound to secrecy. But although it had been the Duchess who had made the promise to the Earl, she herself had been included in the promise, and as at the time she made no protest she could not now tell herself that she had not been party to the assurance of secrecy which her protectress had made to his lordship the Earl of Brockheath.

The Marquis, who had said the previous evening that they would ride this morning, now asked her if she still wished to do so. She shook her head, too unhappy to speak, and after an awkward silence she excused herself and went out into the garden where, passing fountains and lily ponds, statuary and immaculately-trimmed hedges and lawns, she found herself in a wild part of the grounds, a part so reminiscent of the gardens at the parsonage that she found tears of homesickness leaping to her eyes. If only she could return to her own home, to the love and comfort of her parents . . . But why not? Beatrix had no need of her – in fact she would welcome Eleanor's departure now that they were no longer friends. As she herself had stated, she had never once really required Eleanor's company.

Once having seen that there were no serious obstacles to her return, Eleanor somehow felt a little better. That she had been so near to finding complete happiness would always be with her, and the memory of the Marquis one which she would cherish for the whole of her life. But that she must marry was without doubt, since she could not much longer continue being a burden on her parents. She had promised her Mama that she would consider one or other of the young gentlemen who, at the assemblies, had shown a marked interest in her, and this she must do.

"But how can I marry anyone else now that I love his lordship so much?" she quivered, her eyes filling with tears. "Oh, Beatrix, why did you go out of your way to hurt me like that? We've been such friends –" Pulling herself up, she rose and continued her walk. It was unprofitable to dwell either on her cousin's spitefulness or on what might have been. But that the Marquis should have the conviction that she was as mercenary as the rest was what pained her most. He would always believe this, and soon he would forget that he had ever loved her and be thankful that he had had such a narrow escape.

On her arrival back at the Hall the Dowager was sitting on the verandah, reading a book. This she dropped on to her knee as Eleanor approached, and a swift smile gathered on the pale dry lips.

"You've not forgotten you should be riding with his lordship, then? I had begun to think you had. Run along, child, and change. He won't want to be kept waiting."

Eleanor stood in silence for a long moment, finding difficulty with what she had to say. Presently, however, she did manage to tell her Grace that she and the Marquis were not intending to ride. And then she added, her words escaping all of a rush,

"Your Grace, I would very much like to go home – by that I mean to Yorkshire."

Her Grace's eyes widened.

"I don't think I understand?" she said with a frown.

"It isn't anything I can discuss with you, ma'am." She began to wonder if any evidence of her tears remained. She should have gone first to her room in order to bathe her eyes, she thought, lowering her long lashes as the Duchess continued to subject her to a most critical scrutiny.

"You can't possibly have quarrelled with my nephew," declared her Grace. "You haven't had time."

"No, your Grace."

The old lady frowned more heavily.

"You're very correct all at once, Eleanor."

"Ma'am . . ." she looked pleadingly at her. "Do you mind if I go to my bedchamber?"

The Dowager shook her head, her eyes kindling strangely.

"Rather than go to your bedchamber, you would be better occupied in confiding in me. Something has happened this morning, between you and his lordship. I haven't yet seen him, but I shall—"

"Ma'am," interrupted Eleanor swiftly, "I beg of you not to delve into anything. His lordship and I—and I—w-we . . ." She could not continue and, turning from her Grace, she sped off towards the french window which opened out on to the verandah. She entered the room, tears streaming down her cheeks, and because she could not see properly she was not aware of his lordship's presence until she had run head-long into him. His supporting arms came around her and for one wild ecstatic moment she stood very still, savouring the bliss of his touch and his nearness before, twisting away, she continued on her way towards the door.

She met Beatrix on her way upstairs but, unable to look at her, much less speak, she brushed unceremoniously past her and went to her room where, overwrought and filled with despair, she flung herself on the bed and wept as if her heart would break.

About a quarter of an hour later there was a gentle tap on the door and, aware how bedraggled she looked with her hair awry and her face swollen and damp from excessive weeping, she cried urgently,

"Go away, Eva! I do not require you for the present."

The door opened; she raised herself with a jerk ... to see his lordship standing there, in the open doorway.

"Oh ..." She stared at him, making no effort to fix her curls or dry her cheeks. "Sir ... this is my bedchamber ..."

He came towards the bed and, reaching down, took hold of her hand and pulled her almost roughly to her feet.

"Why didn't you explain?" he demanded in a furious tone she had never heard him use before – a tone edged with harshness and accusation. "I once threatened to beat you and, madam, I shall carry out my threat now – unless you are very careful!"

She blinked at him, strangely taking no exception to his ungentlemanly way of speaking to her.

"The Duchess," she murmured. "She has divulged the secret?" The Marquis gave a deep, impatient sigh.

"She told me what you yourself could have told me: that you refused the Earl of Brockheath's offer of marriage."

"It was supposed to be a secret, my lord," she told him in a subdued voice, and trying not to wince at the pain of his grip on her wrist. "His lordship begged that we would not breathe a word of his proposal to anyone."

To her amazement he actually shook her.

"Did it not occur to you that there could be extenuating circumstances?" he thundered. "You are not usually so mutton-headed!"

She lifted her head then, and her brown eyes flashed.

"If I am a mutton-head," she said with frigid civility, "I cannot conceive why you should want to marry me!"

He looked glintingly at her.

"Madam," he said, "I would remind you that you're taking a good deal for granted! I have *not* made an offer for you!"

At this reminder she coloured almost painfully.

"No, sir, you haven't." Her voice, although faintly subdued, was still edged with cold civility. "I beg your pardon for my unwarranted assumption!"

"Unwarranted assumption, be damned!" Roughly he pulled her to him, forcing up her face with an imperious gesture of his hand. "Don't adopt that coy and missish attitude with me! You are fully aware that I intended proposing to you!"

"Then why –"

"And don't ask questions at a time like this!" With a mastery that both thrilled and frightened her, he kissed her hard on the mouth. "I warn you, madam, that if you consent to marry me, you will have to change your ways!"

She laughed shakily, and looked up at him through eyes that were starry with happiness yet still wet from her so recently-shed tears of despair.

"Yes, my lord," she replied with assumed meekness.

His lordship laughed then, and said inconsistently,

"No, you shall not change. I wouldn't miss our sparring matches for the world. Do you realize that they will have to take the place of so much entertainment that I have been used to?"

"You mean, sir, that you're intending to live quietly here, in the country?"

"If you marry me, yes." He drew her close to his heart again. "I believe that I have no need to ask if a country life will satisfy you, my love."

She shook her head.

"I shall prefer it to all things," she told him seriously and, when he did not speak, she ventured to ask him what the Duchess had said.

"Only that the Earl had proposed and been rejected."

"I see . . ." She paused a long time. "You were completely satisfied with only that? I mean – my cousin must have made things seem very black against me?"

The Marquis's face became so grim that Eleanor actually shivered in his arms.

"Beatrix just happened to enter the drawing-room when my aunt was explaining – this was after she had forced from me the reason why you were so unhappy. Your cousin would have escaped, when she heard what was being discussed –" His lordship paused a moment and again felt his betrothed shiver in his arms. "However, I prevented her from leaving the room –"

"You did? How?"

A smile of grim amusement touched the fine line of his mouth.

"I merely took hold of her wrist."

"Oh . . ." Instinctively Eleanor rubbed a soothing hand over her own wrist, amazed to see that it was slightly bruised.

"Yes," said his lordship on noting her action. "And I also forced the truth from her, discovering that her words to you had been such that retaliation was forgivable – although," he added with a laugh, "I'm of the firm opinion that your Papa would most strongly condemn me for saying so."

"Indeed, sir, he would!"

"Do you think, my love, that we could both drop the formalities?"

"You mean, my lord, that I call you J-Justin?"

"Yes, Eleanor, I do," he replied and they both laughed.

"Sir – I mean, Justin," she was saying a few minutes later, her locks more awry than ever, "it is not *convenable* for you to be in my bedchamber."

The dark blue eyes lit with amusement.

"So you want me to leave?" he said, holding her from his heart for a space. "You know, my love, if you say yes, I shall have to accuse you of telling me fibs again."

"You're incorrigible!"

"So you have told me before."

"I think, when we are wed, that it is you who will have to change your ways, my lord – I mean – Justin," she added on noting the look of admonition that entered his eyes.

"That is my intention," he said.

"I do not mean in giving up all your London pleasures! I mean that you will have to adopt a more polite and gentlemanly attitude towards me."

"Fustian!"

"But I am a lady, and –"

"You're a hoyden at times, whose manners leave a great deal to be desired!"

"If you persist in provoking me, then you must expect my manners to suffer."

The Marquis laughed and, deciding that no comment was necessary, he brought her to his heart and for long while there was complete silence in the room. But after this interlude he talked to her, seriously now, explaining why he had brought her here.

"The invitation was actually given to my aunt – it had to be," he went on. "But it was given in effect to bring you to my home. You see, dear, men in love often discover that girls they met during the Season in London, perhaps at some ball or in another glamorous and highly romantic setting, are totally different when seen again in the country. I had to be sure – absolutely sure, as marriage for me is forever. I want only one girl; she must give me everything – love, companionship and all else that goes to make a successful union. I must confess that at first I had no notion that I had met the girl I had been searching for ..." He paused on noting her expression. "You have something you wish to say to me?"

She nodded, and after only the smallest hesitation she told him everything – about her own accidental eavesdropping, and then subtly mentioned Beatrix's part, successfully managing not to make it sound anywhere near so reprehensible as it was. In fact, she realized that he had not actually grasped the fact of any *deliberate* eavesdropping because he was so thoughtful, and when he spoke it was to say,

"So you know about the disparaging remarks I made concerning you?" He was frowning heavily and she knew he was angry with himself.

"It doesn't matter," she returned lightly. "After all, you didn't really know me very well at that time." He said nothing, but continued to frown. Eleanor laughed and reminded him that he had said more disparaging things about her to her face. His eyes glimmered then, and his lips twitched.

"So I have," he owned. "You and I are never all politeness towards one another, are we? But this is what makes it all so entertaining," he added when she did not reply. "The usual run of obliging females leaves me totally unmoved."

"You always said I was different –" Eleanor broke off as another tap sounded on the door panel. Before she had time to draw herself from her lover's embrace Eva had entered, and instead of retreating instantly, as both occupants of the room expected, she just stood there, her horrified eyes fixed upon Eleanor's hair.

"Miss," she exclaimed throwing up her hands, "your hair! My lord," she said sternly, walking into the room and looking up into his amused countenance, "I must request you to leave – at once. I cannot have Miss Sherburn looking like that! Her hair must be dressed immediately!"

"Fustian!" returned his lordship blandly. "Miss Sherburn doesn't mind that her hair isn't immaculate –"

"Sir," broke in Eva in dignified tones, "it is for *my* peace of mind that I make my request." And with that she marched back to the door and, holding it open, waited for his lordship to leave the room.

"You don't appear surprised at finding a gentleman in

your mistress's bedchamber," he remarked as he made his way to the door.

"Her Grace has informed me of the betrothal, sir." Eva was all smiles now as she went on to congratulate him. But she did add the hope that his lordship would not make a practice of disarranging her mistress's hair. "You will have realised, sir, that I am an artist?"

"I have indeed."

"And no artist wants to see his or her work destroyed – and for so trivial a reason."

Both Eleanor and his lordship laughed.

"So it's a trivial reason, eh?"

"Yes, sir!"

He had reached the door and he turned, his dark blue eyes alight as they settled on his beloved's face.

"Don't let her keep you long, my dear. I am not a patient man."

"The greater the damage the longer it takes to repair," said Eva inexorably. And then she too laughed. "But I will be as quick as I can," she promised.

"Thank you, ma'am," rejoined his lordship. "I shall expect to see Miss Sherburn in the garden in ten minutes' time."